PRETTY THINGS

by the same author

LIFE AFTER DEATH and other stories
MALINGERING

Pretty Things
by Susan Compo

VERSE CHORUS PRESS   2001

Printed in Canada

FIRST EDITION

ISBN 1-891241-12-5
Library of Congress Catalog Card Number 99-69644

Cover photograph © Stephanie Chernikowski
Book design by Steve Connell

Verse Chorus Press
PO Box 14806
Portland OR 97293
info@versechorus.com

01 02 03 04   10 9 8 7 6 5 4 3 2 1

For Bangs:
not much of a cat, but a
heck of a writing partner

In memory of Ernie Vega

GISELLE ENTWISTLE, proprietor of Crazing—formerly Stage Diving, Inc.—is dejected. All afternoon she's been unable to make a single basket with the waste paper from the rough drafts of press releases she's been trying to write.

With Crazing she personally manages a stable of clients. "Stable" makes her smile, since more often they're not. She guides the careers of some of them, courts and consoles others—a combination agent, PR girl, babysitter, buddy, and lukewarm shoulder. And she's all the while aware that fame, the fate she seeks for them, is a star-crossed path best represented on the side of a souvenir coffee mug.

Her clients range from teen pop idol Adon to a lazy, aspiring country-and-western star named Len Tingle, with whom Giselle regrets having fallen irrevocably in love. In a way she loves all thirteen of them. That they should fail to return the emotion is an inviolate part of the equation. It's as if they have the keys to her city and she, while vaguely aware she should, is helpless to change the lock.

So she carries on, the reliable narrator for someone like Adon's brilliantine career, she being the oldest chick in his little black book. And she holds off the loneliness, the cold bath that sometimes envelops her—often after a conversation with Len, who is Warren Oates in *Dillinger*, in *Bring Me the Head of Alfredo Garcia*, in *Badlands*, in *Two Lane Blacktop*…. In fewer words, he is all she wants in a man and less (which is in effect the same thing as more).

Tonight Giselle is at a party she hadn't wanted to attend. Her subconscious is working the room. Over crudités, she's having to alternately defend and justify Adon, as if she herself had single-handedly shot off this waxy Bazooka Joe. No, she insists, consider the vacuum that conjured him, formed him from stardust and Play-doh melded together like a furball (a little like the universe).

Her protests are halfhearted. She knows that Adon and his teenage-rampage/skateboards-and-love songs pave the way for the rest of the clients. He allows her to handle people like Len, Hedda Hophead… and child star Frances Culligan, who was on the books before she could read and treading the boards barely able to walk. And then there is Vicki Prescott, whose art is doing well, within reason.

Giselle smiles to herself (a magazine editor grins back) and muses over the way that in thrift stores the stationery you'll most often find—still pristinely wrapped in brine-brittle plastic—is party invitations: drawings of pitted olives in martini glasses, skewered hot dogs on brick barbecues. The thought makes her return to Vicki.

VICKI: Kitsch Love

The crochet skirt on the toilet-roll doll was being lifted once again. It was an action that ruled Vicki's life. One day, too, she might get around to adjusting the setting on the toaster so she wouldn't have to submerge the thick white bread two and three times. One dip would do, and they'd spring up framed and picture-perfect, coppertoned as a day at the beach.

She thought about a headline she'd once seen, from a giddy morning TV news team going over the day's stories. *THE BRIDE WILL BE CHANGING HER MIND*, it read; but the story it capped, about a glamour-coated celebrity set to wed a music mogul, had about as much relevance to Vicki's life as the foreign-exchange rates. It wasn't as if she were going anywhere.

It was agoraphobia she thought she had—the fear of long-haired cats, of furry 1950s sweaters. Or was that right? She didn't think it was the fear of heights, but she probably had that, too.

Really, it was the fear of anything out there: words beginning with x, wire handbaskets. Bus stops and railway crossings and fat power lines. Powder rooms and knitting needles and anything that didn't meet her precise, mail-order expectations.

Vicki turned on the clock-radio while she ironed, her water-filled 7-Up bottle providing a bouquet of what would become steam. She hummed as she listened to Herb Alpert and his Tijuana Brass.

That night, she knew, her husband had invited his boss for dinner. Vicki, for whom baked Alaska was a rather tasty relief map, would be expected to think fast. She had all day to decide, but knew she could only turn to Candida, her wise and knowing neighbor.

When she'd last seen her, Candida had had two plastic salad bowls cupped to her iceberg-breasts, the successful culmination of a Tupperware party hosted by a nubile young man. Candida's friends had applauded the wild divorcée's coup, and her ingenuity in having a lone male captive in command in the women's domain.

Vicki's own relationship to the others in and around her cul-de-sac was mostly tenuous; she held back, assumed the affect of a scarecrow-size sunflower.

She put her bare feet into her closed-toe, pointed mules. The reaches of her ski pants lapped up the soles, which curled like parched tongues. Then she flipped the ends of her hair far better than she would any pancake or pizza.

Candida rejoiced to see Vicki's feet tottering on her *Now Wipe Your Feet* doormat.

"Get in here, girl!" Candida enthused, bear-hugging her. "I just made a coffee cake." Inside, her red nails castaneted against the airtight Quonset hut of a camouflage-green recipe file.

When Vicki returned home, she was laden with supplies from Candida, who'd called after her in farewell: "Don't forget next week, and our GTO!" GTO meant Girls' Night Out—Candida took it from '60s rock vamps Girls Together Outrageously, which she was once nearly part of, or so she claimed.

Vicki vacuumed, her hair wrapped in a Daisy Mae bandanna. She cooked, resting a spoon in a turquoise dish shaped like a chicken. She took a bath, with foam poured out of a plastic champagne bottle.

Tony, Vicki's husband, returned and moved through the house with a kind of sullen oblivion. "A prince among geeks," Vicki's mother had called him. The cat with no pajamas. But Vicki, certain she knew which side of the blanket she was buttered on, stuck to him like the kimono she wore to greet him now. The ostrich feathers on her slippers tickled like a sneeze. To please him, she would do anything.

Tony brushed her off and sat in his chair. Vicki wanted to say she was thinking of taking night classes, but she was afraid: afraid to go to the college, afraid of her idea.

After his martini, Tony showered. The boss came and his cotton-candy wife asked Vicki if she needed any help. "I'm fine," Vicki replied, as she stirred instant mashed potatoes. The meal was unsuitable; the wet bar got soaked. Its surface warped like a crater.

Vicki got ready for bed, washing her face and then not applying moisturizer, as if she were a preteen again. In bed, Tony turned on his side, away from her—but he always did that.

"It's over," he said suddenly. "I've found someone else." He never raised his voice.

The mirror behind the bar became a target for all the glasses Vicki had collected secondhand—glasses buried in detergent boxes, or awarded after full tanks at gas stations. The elastic of her see-through underwear sagged and protruded like Medusa worms. She felt like a Viewmaster replaced by a carousel slide-projector; she felt like a joke.

"I'll give you time to find your feet," Tony told Vicki. He'd tracked her to where she lay curled on the plastic-protected sofa in the living room they seldom entered. Her slippers were huddled together, neat for her feet when she got up.

Vicki went to Candida's the next day but forgot to return what she'd borrowed. She didn't say anything about Tony. That weekend, at the porno karaoke outing Candida had cooked up, Vicki was the reluctant, electric volunteer who interacted with the video screen. Her fear, like her panties, gave way. Her breasts in a push-up bra were so sweet, the one on the left slightly larger than the one on the right. She was away, and now, in front of a group of strangers, she thought only of Tony.

"You have to watch the shy ones," one of Candida's friends said.

"That was quite a performance," Candida added. Vicki didn't react. "Are you okay?"

"Tony's left me," she replied in Tony's exact volume of voice.

"There, there," Candida replied. "We'll get you back on your feet."

A Mayflower moving van took Vicki not far away. Soon, at her evening art class, her weakly bearded teacher was scolding her. The images she created were trite, their sentiments cloying like lace eyelets on glass curtains. But she went back to her small apartment feeling neither chastened nor empty. Years later, she'd be asked to exhibit some of her work in a show; the kitsch theme wouldn't matter then. Her thick macramé butterflies and glossy, pond-eyed frogs would hang alongside doughy puppy dogs and striped street urchins wise beyond their years.

STREAKED IN CHENILLE the next morning, Giselle is still thinking of Vicki as she drinks strong decaffeinated coffee kept fresh in a plastic container. What became of this Tupperware man Vicki had mentioned? And more importantly, did he need representation? TV on, she riffles through her thoughts and they appear like a blizzard of calendar pages speeding up the plot in a 1940s movie, although it is now resolutely 1990. Aside from contacting Vicki, she must 1) get back to her cat-book author; and 2) put out feelers about Them Park, an ambitious project of Perry Walker's, to do with creating a rock-and-roll theme park.

But dealing with Perry means dealing with Pandra, a rock-and-roll mistress—now the aspiring author of a book about herself and the 1970s glitter-rock days in Los Angeles. Giselle doesn't feel up to it today: she thinks Pandra plays a kind of tops and bottoms to her own life: at times chastising Giselle for so flagrantly missing out, then turning around and reassuring her that if, in fact, she had, it was probably for the best. Pandra was the kind of girl who had style, too, while the most Giselle could come up with was to be color-coordinated.

Pandra and Giselle had started their careers in similar ways: they were both office girls for entertainment-related companies, although Pandra, as a phone clerk, had a more dubious connection. Giselle had been Girl Friday to the manager of a ghoulish rock star, Dominic, who was blood pellet–drenched on stage and vodka-soaked (at the 19th Hole on the grounds of the country club) off it. What began as a menial job—a baptism by filing—soon grew to embrace Giselle's talents. The press releases she wrote were trumpeted by her boss as being of the *Alice in Wonderland* school of imperatives: *Read Me*, they implored.

She also had a gift for nabbing public-domain art. Sketches of archaic printing presses and Victorian rabbits in heart-emblazoned vests were applied in a manner that made them seem contemporary, with just the right hue of nostalgia—a brand of inventiveness that implied something new and exciting.

Giselle wasn't a Girl Friday for long, and following a stint as an A&R person for A&M Records, she returned to PR. Alphabet soup, she'd laughed to herself, was her primordial ooze (and basted her to this day). *Mmm Mmm Good.* One of her clients had been a rock-and-roll group in need of push. As it was no good heralding sex or drug excesses in the mid-'80s, she set about planting a story that the band, Love Thing, refused to have brown or green M&Ms in their backstage catering bowls. Soon people who knew nothing else about the band latched onto this innocent detail, with its near-Warholian wink. The candy manufacturer was believed to have launched a special edition tie-in bag, minus the offending colors.

At home today, Giselle sips. After one more coffee, she'll head for her Selma Avenue offices in downtown Hollywood. Her first call will be to Sidonia Burne, her cat author. Sidonia's book, *Pet Project*, is subtitled *Bedtime Stories for Cats* and has a special feature—a bound-in ribbon bookmark designed to keep a feline listener rapt.

Cats sleep 20 hours a day, Giselle's copy reads. *Why not give 'em something to dream about?* Giselle's assistant, Violet Strood, bounds into the office.

"Sorry I'm late. I just got back from the Mojave Desert. I went to a shopping mall. It was great. What do you need done?"

"It's quiet so far. But your mentioning the desert makes me think of this manuscript I'm in a quandary about."

"Is that anything like a quarry?" Violet asks.

"Well, it does have to do with rock."

"Ugh."

"I know your views on pop, Strood. You've made them known to me more than once. But there's more to this story than big hair and funny clothes."

"What, for instance?"

"A rock star's strange disappearance. And Pandra seems to be the only one left who was there when he died…."

"Now you're talking," Violet says as Giselle opens a file cabinet to retrieve a fat manila folder.

"Whenever you have a chance," Giselle explains. "I wouldn't want to interfere with your shopping."

"You know, they even run special buses to that mall. You ought to go."

"Thanks, but I like to think of myself as still being on the fighting side of support hose, plastic handbags, and organized bus trips."

"Sorry. I'll let you know by the end of the week." Violet balances the manuscript like a mortarboard on her croptop head; the envelope tips as she turns for the partition doorway.

"I see you'll never make Homecoming Queen."

"Me? I was expelled from finishing school."

"Then you might like the book after all." Giselle turns her attention to her in-tray, cracks open a demo cassette by a band called the Glee Club. She stuffs it into her deck and starts to read, then puts down, a pitch from Hedda Hophead. The Glee Club, Giselle considers, might have some use. Judging by their

5x8 glossies they're more Four Freshmen than Four Horsemen, and this could come in handy, taking in the girls still too young for Adon's impending goatee phase.

For her part, Violet gathers the list of calls to make, puts it in one corner of her ramshackle desk and starts to read the rock-and-roll manuscript. She wears a rubber thumb in case she wants to turn the pages with something approximating speed.

CHARM SCHOOL DROPOUT
by Pandra Jane Walker

"Pandra was put out to pasture in June of 1988. How fondly she remembered those fields, and dancing all night in them!"

Pandra is repeating these words to herself as she walks in flat grass in the second Summer of Love. She sidesteps the debris—tin cans, foil, plastic silverware—and escapes the music festival pinned like a dime-store breastplate brooch to the strand of costume jewelry that is the Las Vegas strip. Pandra avoids the tie-dyed revelers, ignores the hooded stage, and steps into a cool, close tent where she will learn not her future but her past.

It is a den of false memory, just as her family rumpus room once was.

Xenia, a young woman with copper hair and segmented slivers of bracelets augmenting both arms, proffers a pack of holy cards, a bashful flush, and half-gazes into a jaundiced glass ball. She giggles, an arthritic chortle. "What is your question?"

Pandra brushes back her blanched-wheat hair. "I don't have one, really," she says. "Well, I was wondering... do you think I could have murdered someone?"

Xenia takes Pandra's left hand, observes her chipped and quick-torn fingernails. "I see in your half-moons a contest," Xenia says, affecting transfixion. "A contest not for usual beauty...."

And the sphere's clouds clear to Pandra, years ago, rubbing her eyes in the smoggy rain. She is stopped in her car, looking out the passenger window. At curb level she spies a silver platform boot of an impossible height. She follows the boot to find a boy whose hair, too, appears stilted. His peacock clothes are topped with a long feather boa. With him is a girl in satin hot pants and star-shaped Lolita sunglasses.

"Glitter people," Pandra mutters, as she heads back to the locked inland of suburbia.

Then, in fish-eye focus, the hippie-swirled facade of the Odyssey Theater appears in the now-prismed ball. Psychedelic paint covers what was once the Earl Carroll Theater, whose confiding proscenium once promised *Through These Portals Pass the Most Beautiful Girls in the World*. Today, scores of hopefuls snake down the Deco steps towards the littered parking lot, each hoping to end up cheekbone to shoulder with David Bowie's *Pin-Ups* persona on a Sunset Strip billboard.

Scouts from KCAT-FM survey the line and select at random a short stack of possibles who pass, like sugary ghosts in filmic tat, on through to backstage, where they'll be caught and photographed as their reflections leer in suggestively protruding bulb-framed mirrors. Then the "probables" move on to a camp circle of folding chairs where Pandra, in her diamond-hemmed scarf skirt, charm bracelets, earrings, shoulderless top, and glossy platform shoes, recognizes Mona Best and the boy, Chuckie, today wearing a silent-era cowboy shirt and calling himself Chuck Wagon.

Pandra has had to bid her friend Topaz good-bye on the steps outside, by the card tables, where a brisk young woman, bracing as sunburn balm, asked Pandra her details.

"Name?"

"Pandra."

"Is that Miss, Mrs. or Ms.? Or," she hesitated, "Mister?"

"Misc.!" Topaz had leapt in. "Got that? M-I-S-C." She eyes Pandra. "Knock 'em dead kid," she pronounces by way of farewell. Topaz considers Pandra's feet. "I would say break a leg, but..." and she walks off toward the parking lot.

So Pandra finds herself in the coterie of "probables." She looks over at Mona, who glares back and sticks out her tongue, just like the decal on her denim and metal-studded jacket. At Mona's exaggerated feet is a boxer dog; his right eye is circled in kohl eyeliner.

A man in a satin bomber jacket stands at the top of the circle. "Hello," he says. "I'm Jeff Banks, morning manager here at KCAT. That's morning as in This Is Overtime. But, hey, it's worth it just to get a look at all you crazy people. Now then, just a few words before I turn you over to Karen from RCA, who in turn will pass you along to Lori. We're judging you today primarily at face value. Now I know that may sound shallow..."

The group, puzzled, fails to react. How else would you judge someone?

"But we'll also try to look a little bit deeper so as not to be superficial." Jeff sinks into the recessed heels of his Earth shoes. "So it's important you show us your inner sparkle, your dazzle, your razz-ma-tazz. Let us see what makes you the ultimate, consummate glitter rocker. That's really what's on trial here."

"Hey, no one said nothing about a trial," a girl named Ava Lance calls out. "Don't I get to call my lawyer?"

"Well, maybe 'trial' isn't exactly the right word," Jeff concedes. "But what we want to do is test you, ask you a couple of questions, have a look at your right profile…"

"I don't have a wrong one," says Chuckie, drawing no laughs.

"And assess your costumes."

"Costumes!" shrieks Chuckie. "What's he talking about, costumes? I look like this seven days a week, 24 hours a day. Unless I'm undressed," he winks. "Then I'm even more outrageous."

"I'd get the crap kicked out of me if I looked like this all the time in La Milagra," says another guy. "You're just lucky."

"Fine," says Jeff. "Now let me turn you over—"

"Whoo!" choruses the crowd.

"—to Karen Espinoza from RCA." Karen, also in stock satin and rubber-soled shoes, toughly eyes the group.

"Now, if it were up to me," she begins, "I'd say you were all winners. But as you know, there can only be one. I also want to stress that although it'll be your face that will adorn the most famous billboard stretch in the world—after you sign a release form, of course—and while David will certainly know about you and be very proud of you, at no time, and I repeat, *at no time*, will you come into contact with him."

"Oh, I've had contact," Mona says in a stage whisper. "Believe you me, I've had contact *and* liftoff."

"So on behalf of David and RCA I'd like to thank you all for coming today and for being fans. Thank you." A weak applause sends Karen off as Jeff returns.

"Okay. What happens now is we'll call you out one by one onto the stage, at random…"

"What, no lineup?" Ava asks.

"And Lori will ask you a couple of quick questions. So while you're waiting, have a seat, feel free to check the mirrors, and help yourselves to coffee and doughnuts."

"I knew the LAPD had a hand in this!" laughs Ava, setting off the entire group. "It's not the vice squad, is it?"

"In short, have a good time and take it easy," says Jeff.

"Take it easy?" Chuckie repeats, sarcasm-drenched. "Sure, man."

"Imagine telling a bunch of glitter kids to check the mirrors," Mona says to Pandra. "That's like telling me to remember to swallow when I'm giving head. I'm Mona, by the way."

"Pandra."

"How come I've never seen you before?"

"I'm new," Pandra manages, as if she's just transferred from a different school.

"Well, then," Mona says, encompassing Pandra with her straggly ostrich boa, "let me show you the ropes."

From their vantage point behind the curtain, a spot Mona refers to in passing as "backstage, my home away from home," the contestants crane and strain to overhear each other's onstage answers. Suddenly, Chuckie storms back and slams down his satin cowboy hat onto the sculpted seat of a folding chair.

"I don't have a whore's chance in heaven," he moans. "There's no way they're gonna put this boy up on that billboard with that boy. After all we do, and it's still 1973. I'm

20

not even gonna stick around to get asked to leave." And he disappears out the back, through a propped-open fire exit.

"That's a mistake," Mona says to Pandra. "Though God knows I'm not going to be the one to try and stop him. It's so typical of him, quitting too soon. He probably even denies himself orgasms. Oh, well, never mind. My guess is that our main competition is that Ava chick. She's funny, she's outrageous, she's black—and Bowie likes black chicks. But the only way she'll win is by tripping over my dead body."

"Mona Best?" asks a man with a clipboard and a gym-style whistle.

"Good luck!" Pandra calls from where she sits with the three other remaining entrants, Ava among them. Mona drags the boxer along on his leash. Then the small group listens to Mona run through her credits: *Star* Magazine, a paragraph in the People section of *Time*, a mention in *Viva*, a photograph of her hitching to see the New York Dolls in *Groupie News*, her modeling turn with Cyrinda Foxe. But the questions, asked by Lori Lightsout of *Lori after Dark* in her deep-seated dulcet voice, remain inaudible. Just as Pandra is about to catch one word of a question, Mona's back.

"Piece of cake," she says, sprawling onto the unwelcoming chair. "She asked me things like, Who is my role model? and I said, Frances Farmer... *after*. I think she liked that. See, I didn't let her boring appearance fool me. She looks like some kind of radical women's-libber, but I think she really hates all that feminist shit."

Ava gets up for her turn and Mona says, "I've seen snails move better."

"Look, amoeba-brain," Ava strikes. "Who are you calling snail? Got a mirror that's not covered in lines? You're the snail, honey. You've left your trail of slime all over this town. I can always tell if Mona's been there. It's like the red carpet's been laid out: red carpet all right, a Slip and Slide!"

"At least I get there first," Mona hisses, but Pandra is distracted, wondering how to answer the questions. Her role models? None. Ideas? Zero. When it's finally her turn, she totters out, a Wendy reluctant to leap off the sill. The lights on her are so bright, Lori herself so off-putting in her bulky black sweater-dress.

What answers Pandra gives, she's asked to repeat. "I don't know," she says. "I'm not sure." In response to the role-model question, she says the only thing she's thought out. "I like the Gene Tierney character in *Leave Her to Heaven*."

"Really?" says Lori. "I'm not familiar with that one. Why did you pick her?"

"Oh!" Pandra is suddenly animated. "She's really determined and possessive. She's driven by her love for her dead father, and she kills her husband's brother, a crippled kid, by making him swim too far. He was so irritating, anyway. And then there's this scene where she's riding horseback in New Mexico, swinging an urn containing her father's ashes, against this matte-postcard sky and it's just… incredible."

"I'm, uh, sure it is." In deejay lingo, the *uh*, Pandra knows, must be choreographed. Professionals like Lori don't stumble. "Any other icons?"

"Aurora in *Sleeping Beauty*?" Pandra guesses, treading on another taboo, a fairy tale. Unfortunately for Pandra, she has failed to spot Lori's *NOW* button.

"Thanks, Pandra. That'll do you."

Pandra expects Lori to add, "Don't call us, we'll call you" as she walks backstage, sizing up her endless future as a telephone-answering girl. Jeff reappears and announces the two finalists, parodying a game-show host. "Mona Best, come on down. And Ava Lance, your price is right."

"How do you know?" Ava wonders aloud.

Jeff says, "The rest of you are welcome to watch these two ladies battle it out." But Pandra can't face it. As the others go into the hall to sit where an audience might, Pandra prepares to leave, heading for the dressing room to collect her Biba makeup bag. Walking in, she stumbles upon Mona in a skin-tight Our Gang T-shirt, hot pants, and platform boots, bending over and sprinkling something into Ava's shoes.

"What are you doing here?" Mona hisses. "I thought you were a goner."

In place of answering, Pandra simply collects her bag and leaves. She walks behind the building to find Topaz and tell her the news.

"But Mona wasn't anything like you said," Pandra insists. "She was really nice to me until she got weird at the end. She even told me some of the questions."

"Mona? Nice?" Topaz pauses. "What's wrong with this picture?"

"It's true. She said Lori would ask about role models and that she wasn't that big on feminism. Those were the only questions I did good at."

"Wait a minute, wait a minute. Roll back the tape. She told you Lori wasn't a feminist? Pandra, where have you been? She's always harping on about women's lib!"

"Are you sure? I mean, at the end I even saw Mona putting foot powder in Ava's boots."

"Oh, forget about it now. We tried. If you want, let's go back to my place and listen to Silverhead."

"I probably should head back," Pandra says. "I have to work tomorrow."

"First though, let's swing by Famous Amos for some munchies. Have you ever met him?"

"Who?"

"Amos? On Sunset? You know that place with a big cookie?"

"Oh, that. I thought it was a pizza."

"Some weird pizza. No, he's cool. He used to be an agent but he got sick of it so he bakes cookies instead."

They park and walk into the tiny store, decorated with macramé plants and a carved wood sign reading *Free Smells*. Amos, in a silk Hawaiian shirt, greets Topaz warmly.

"We need to lift our spirits," she says, explaining about the contest.

"You girls are great," he replies. "You should get yourselves an act. The Bowiemians. I'm serious. You girls are dynamite."

And then a slate gray appears. In the parking lot of the Woodlawn Motel, Mona's curled, a Googie crescent on the filthy floor of a phone booth, surrounded by a reef of aquarium rock–size broken glass. She doesn't stir.

Pandra uses her hands and hair to cover her face in the airless tent.

"I wouldn't worry," says Xenia. "It was a long time ago."

"What, what do I owe you?"

"Nothing," says Xenia. "You paid at the beginning, remember?"

Pandra's name is, and always was, Pandra. Her last name, too, was funny: Jane as in plain. Just Jane, not Janes, and no, it's not her middle name.

Her family lived in a small home in Orange County, California. Their house was like the shoebox crafts you made in grammar school, with a cellophane window where the heel would be. If you looked in, you'd see Pandra, her mom, her sister, her father about as dimensional as crayoned cutouts with Popsicle sticks for spines.

You'd see them gathered, together for once, on a Sunday evening to watch the *Ed Sullivan Show*. Ellen fidgeted in discomfort over the sight of Topo Gigio, a puppet mouse, and her mother also feigned disgust. Her father quietly slipped out of the room to go to his sanctuary place, the garage.

Pandra didn't say a word; in fact she secretly preferred the manic, large-eared mite to the four lads from Liverpool who came after, eliciting such a frenzy.

Today, if Pandra could have remembered the nasal tune the tiny puppet shrieked she would have taken it to a desert island. It would make a theme tune to accompany her, along with significant bits of her life that would follow on behind her like a conga line.

Pandra sat down at her computer, which was covered in paper roses. She personalized all her possessions in some way, thus augmenting herself. She prepared to work on her book, drawing thoughts close around her like starched bedcovers. But then she twisted and turned: some days more than others, one needed to be in love.

And Pandra was, truly and redoubtably. But not with Perry, to whom she'd spoken her vows with something like regret. The day she married him, the morning tabloids cried

THE BRIDE WILL BE CHANGING HER MIND. They were right, though it took her a while to realize it.

She'd always been able to resist depression. She was fortunate that way, the kind of person who asked to be born. That light has bathed her as it would a cherub, bottle-capping her with a Byzantine tinfoil nimbus. Even in the Christmas play, she was the herald angel—the one with the scoop.

When in *The Wizard of Oz* the Wicked Witch condemned Dorothy to die once the sands in the gargoyle-gnarled timepiece had run through, Pandra couldn't help thinking, Who'd ever want to go back to black and white?

Black and white to her meant the earliest she could remember, a hazy screened-in service porch of time spent in California's Central Valley. She used to swing sideways in the schoolyard, humming torch songs like "The End of the World" while flailing her little legs in anguished empathy. Two years in a row she did this: once, she slammed into the steel-candy-cane side pole and knocked herself flat out. A year later, abruptly airborne. she fell out of the swing. Both incidents were on the eve of her class photo, so for two years running she had a black target to show for her right eye, prompting the playground cry, "Pandra the Panda!"

But by that second year she'd convinced her classmates the center swing was haunted and for weeks it sat motionless, stirred only by the spirit-world breeze.

That had taught her the power of a well-told tale.

Soon after, her family left their central California home for the promised land of Orange County. Her sister stopped watching *American Bandstand* (it belonged to a dust-bowl past) and turned instead to *Hullabaloo*, *Boss City*, and *Where the Action Is!*—all go-going concerns.

Pandra's mother, Audrey, signed her younger daughter up for a scout troop, the Busy Bees, and threatened Pandra with charm school. For her it *was* the end of the world, until Ellen discarded yet another toy, a naked Barbie doll.

About the time her mother forced her on and into the Busy Bees, Pandra was also feeling the pangs of preteendom, responding with shocks and shards of denial teamed with defiance. Her carriage was also an issue: she'd fashioned a deliberately poor posture.

"You walk like you're following a plow," her mom would scold, promising her she'd end up on Tobacco Road, surviving on grits and dirty water. There were great songs connected with those elements, so Pandra didn't mind. But Mrs. Jane hatched a plan that involved Pandra parading nightly with books atop her seemingly round head. One day the girl grabbed her confirmation Bible, knowing that when it inevitably fell to earth, she would have sinned and subsequently be freed from the obligation.

It worked; she was grounded.

Pandra's family lived in the snug of an unincorporated, nooselike cul-de-sac, in a house with worm-rotted wood floors that her mother insisted were superior to the neighbors' tract-home cement. Pandra envied others their wall-to-wall carpets, their skating sidewalks. When she ventured out on roller skates, it was over chunks of asphalt and root-risen granite. It might have been character-building, but she wasn't interested in scaling Mount Rushmore.

What she was interested in was clothes—and as her classmates started turning up in go-go boots, pint-sized dancing girls in birdcages, Pandra wanted the shoes, too. But they proved elusive at Sears, at Woolworth's. Then, at a garage sale, she found some drill-team boots. She promptly tore off the strippers' tassels, pared them down to sixties sharpness, and wore them proudly to school the next day, putting them on halfway there so her mom wouldn't know. Pandra's classmates laughed at her, but she got her own back later, wearing the shoes as a cheerleader while they sat sullen on the sidelines.

Until that triumph she retreated, watching the nighttime TV serials and consoling herself with words intended to be spoken by fully formed adult dolls. The first fan letter Pandra wrote was to a distraught television character who'd jumped off a cliff into frothing foam. The reply she received was a picture-postcard of the show's cast, minus the character she'd written to.

At the end of the year, her mother received a fan letter about Pandra, following her appearance as an angel in a nativity play. *Just to let you know how tickled I was when little Pandra burst in and shouted "Behold! And no!"* So it was her mother decided to enroll her daughter in a charm school, one conducted by a store best known for its mail-order catalogs.

Pandra had been dismissed from the Busy Bees—wings stripped for conspiring to enlist other girls in her schemes. The prank that finished her off was a midnight trip en masse to the mysterious concrete toilets that bookended their beach (a man-made campsite).

Charm school was no more successful; she was soon ousted for refusing to comb her hair. "You're a bad seed!" her mother yelled, with more resignation than conviction. From then on Pandra never wore her hair in Patty McCormick–style braids, just in case.

Pandra got up from her desk, stretched, and scribbled a few lines on the back of a preaddressed payment envelope, referring to herself by name as usual. *It used to be, when Pandra was alone,* she wrote, *anywhere, or even with someone who less than engaged her, she'd always imagine a lover holding and kissing her, making her. She's got that now.*

So if you buy this book to see both Pandra and your idealized self in it, as in a compact, take care—and maybe we can get along.

Pandra paused and remembered a recurrent dream in which she picked up the phone in the dead heart of night and heard voices in conversation, a turn-of-the-skewed-century party line she hadn't been invited onto. They spoke of the daughter she'd given up, recounting how she fled for home straight afterwards, in order to fall apart surrounded by childhood things in her sickly green bedroom.

The family excursion to the hardware store was intended to be a tribute to each child's individualism. Pandra's sister chose to paint her room a yellow that matched a condiment container. Pandra herself picked a lime green, the color of envy. Their mother shrugged: her daughters, she sighed, just thought too much.

Pandra's primary trust back then was still in the dolls, the Barbies. More precisely it was in the stories she'd develop for them, threaded and darned like the pie-shaped rugs her grandmother had made for their homes, their apartments.

Eventually her mother took the opposing side and told her she was too old to be playing with dolls, and would have to stop. It was worse than the day her class had had a sex-education film at school, about menstruation. When Pandra's ten-year-old boyfriend walked her home that afternoon, he asked her what film the girls had seen, and if he could look at the booklet he was sure had been handed out.

"I ain't got it," Pandra replied and trembled for days after, mainly because she'd said the word *ain't*.

The transition into teen years was even more awkward than learning to feign interest in the September issue of *Seventeen* magazine. Pandra cut her hair like Twiggy's; unwashed, it stuck to her head like a swimming cap. In her freshman year she decided she should behave less intelligently. It was an idea that was fast becoming as outdated as her hairstyle.

Her dunce status was confirmed when the homeroom teacher made her sit in the corner as the daily bulletin was broadcast by an office helper—a job that used to be Pandra's. One day's news featured an announcement of cheerleader try-outs, and she silently vowed to throw her dunce cap into the ring.

Making it onto the squad changed her outlook forever. Pandra still had her cheerleading skirt, its pennant-hem waving and beckoning her back while her letter-sweater whispered from her closet.

The white shoes she wore were regulation issue, eradicating the grade-school laughter at her homemade go-go boots. Her classmates didn't dare snigger at her, now that the team's fortunes and the school's reputation rested in her wrists, changing sides with her star-crossed pom-poms. Her popularity rose with each Friday-night leap.

As Pandra rebuffed numerous advances from boys, her name cropped up on bathroom walls and torn corners of telephone directories. It was a tribute to her, a hostility fueled by the potency of her rejection. She had triumphed. Her family was proud, her friends legion. But Pandra herself was drifting away again. Nominated for Homecoming Queen, she had a surprise in store.

"Pandra!" her mother had called, and her daughter descended the ladder from the attic/crawlspace—as if she'd already won Homecoming, as if she'd been stringing stars up there rather than culling through her box of Barbie things, looking for a dress to copy.

"Yes?" Pandra was forbidden to reply *What?*

"Would you like to watch a movie on TV with me tonight? There's a good one on, about surfing and boys. We could have TV dinners."

Pandra, if she thought about it at all, was entirely indifferent to surfing; still, she was caught by the poignancy of her mother's request, and said yes.

Her mother preheated the oven and peeled back the foil to expose the TV dinners' desserts, and she and Pandra settled in to watch the news, and then the movie. The film documented the lazy yet loving quest of two young men for the perfect wave.

The next day, as Pandra walked home from school, the driver of a VW van flurried his hand at her like a blown-out ocean wave. He was blond, tan, and easily dressed in a silk Hawaiian shirt. Pandra returned her eyes to the slim books she carried.

When she got home she scanned her closet, and the Barbie dresses she'd tucked into her unworn shoes. Nothing suited her Homecoming night: she didn't want to look like a prom queen. She went to Ellen's room and asked if she'd drive her to a vintage-clothing shop.

At Gasoline Alley, her sister bought a pair of patched jeans, while Pandra opted for a cream-colored Depression daydream vision, a Jean Harlow–style floor-length silk gown.

When she tried it on she felt like someone else: herself, for the first time.

Her classmates listened to Led Zeppelin and the Rolling Stones; she began to emulate Joni Mitchell. Almost overnight, Pandra became a local Lady of the Canyon, showing an interest in the guitar, the piano, and—strangest of all—nature and natural things.

She wore a tracing-paper touch of makeup on Homecoming night and her date, a quiet boy named Mark, drove her onto the field in his parents' Lincoln Continental. She stood among the other princesses, a soft silk in a cluster of polyester.

At the ceremony where she was named Queen, she refused the flowers as dead and persecuted things. "Furthermore, I reject the rhinestone crown and the whole sporto ethic of this landlocked school. And I ask each of you to look into your souls where you'll see that there's more to life than school, TV, parties, beer, and cheerleaders."

In the shocked and invigorated crowd that night, on the visitors' bleachers, was Tracy Mixx, who'd waved at Pandra from the van a few days before. That first sight of him had been a premonition. Much later, at a Stephen Stills concert, she would squirm and revolt against the song "Love the One You're With." It was the line, "There's a girl right next to you/and she's just waiting for something to do." Pandra would look at the drab, plaid, shaggy male beside her and cringe. It would serve to propel her, platform feet first, into glam-rock.

But before discovering glitter, she would shed her school-girl confectionery for the striped sand and stripped-down sea.

Pandra's favorite beach at this time was the left-alone shore of San Onofre that lay between stately San Clemente and sleazy Oceanside. Its pristine beaches were open to those with a military connection (Pandra's father was a retired Marine) on days when the troops weren't practicing coastal maneuvers.

Pandra would drive the 50 or so miles in her energy crisis–flouting Chevy Nova, in pursuit of a new, truer life. Her appearance remained fixed in the ideal of her era: she was Long Hair Parted in the Middle. She bought a kneeboard, a sawn-off surfboard, at the Frog House in Newport Beach. Years later, the Bride of Frankenstein scars on her knees still bore witness.

Hopscotch fashion, she leapt over her high-school years, as if her marker were thrown on their numbers: '70, '71, '72.

Cinematically disaffected on campus now, she fell in not with the smoke-as-punctuation/prop, bathroom-dwelling delinquents but with a teenager who dressed like a doll. The girl wore short, aproned dresses underscored by tulip-shaped clogs. She sported rouged cheeks bordered by two Pippi-plaits that petered out near her pointed chin.

Far from being the object of ridicule, Debbie Taunt was the most feared girl on campus, for all four years. Her evocative name was real, she swore. "My mom knew I was special," she'd explain, her eyes like steel balls in a child's hand-held plastic maze.

Her Shirley Temple dresses sometimes yielded to sexy period jersey and crepe, and as Pandra watched from the playing-field sidelines, perched on her stupid stool, she observed and then copied this look for her Homecoming stand.

Pandra knew the other girl knew, and that she wouldn't like it.

Pandra wanted to be her friend.

The girls took Biology class together. It was taught by Mr. Fay, a hunchbacked man who was all of four feet five inches tall. So benign was his nature that the students never put together the sinister cliché of his image and the subject he taught.

The week the class was due to dissect sand sharks, Pandra asked to be paired with Debbie, who was also beginning to waver toward the beach life—for the boys and for the fashion.

Pandra herself would never have such trivial motives. She liked what the ocean represented: relatively unspoiled nature, suburbia's finite end. The beach sensibility was also tied to a fading hippie ethic of noncommercialism.

Shortly before the dissection class, Pandra told Debbie she refused to cut up one of Mother Ocean's creatures, however dead and overpreserved. Debbie smiled her thin-lipped child-star smile.

"I like that." Her voice, even in approval, was petulant.

"We could make a stand," Pandra insisted.

"We could ditch," Debbie replied, her eyes gleaming now like tidepool jewels.

"But we'd have to make our point first," Pandra stressed. "I wish we could take the sharks back to the beach and release them."

"It won't do them as much good as it'd do us. You'd be better off introducing my parents to a new idea or an original experience. They're just as pickled as those sharks."

Pandra was puzzled. It was hard to picture the independently formed Debbie having parents at all. Schoolyard legend held that her older brother, Tom, was a brilliant artist and already making an impression at Disneyland, where he worked. The age gap between Tom and Debbie was great, and she dwelled in his shadow.

In summer Debbie had a job that was equally awe-inspiring. This lacy rayon slip of a girl appeared twice nightly in Disneyland's Electrical Parade, tottering along as Tweedledum. She had *tried out* for the part. And she had landed it. True, Pandra had been a cheerleader till she ceremoniously threw it off, but that was nothing. Anyone with the teeniest bit of determination and teenage girlish grit could do that. But to be a working part of something like *Disneyland*—however plastic and commercial—was beyond belief.

Even out of her Tweedledum costume, Debbie Taunt seemed larger than life. But Pandra found the courage to persevere, to make her point about the sharks. She had to stand up to Debbie, a girl for whom a good pose counted for more than morals.

So Pandra kept on. "What if I stood in front of the class... No, wait. I'll ask Mr. Fay if I can address the class. He's cool—he'll let me. What I'll do is, I'll bring my Bunsen burner up with me and signal to you to get the lights, to turn them off. Then I'll stand there, you know, like an avenging angel. I'll wear all white and I'll tell the class why we cannot, we should not use these gentle creatures for our own useless ends."

Debbie said nothing. Then, finally, "I'm impressed."

"You are?"

"Yes. You mean to tell me you can actually get your Bunsen burner to light?"

Instead, the day before they were due to dissect the sharks, Pandra explained the dilemma to Mr. Fay, who softly gave them passes to the library for the week, thus nullifying their protest. Once there, they signed in, looked at a few outdated issues of *Surfer* magazine, and then snuck out to Jack in the Box for fish sandwiches.

Pandra's pro-animal stance firmly in place, she faced yet another challenge. Her senior prom loomed like a spinster's web.

At the River Jetty Surf Meet in Newport Beach, Pandra sat (at Debbie's decree) directly on the sand. A chair or even a towel beneath her would have been a barrier between herself and nature. When the meet was over and Mike Purpos had won, Debbie and Pandra entered the board-cleared water to body-surf. Pandra wore a dainty strand of dewdrop-size pearls that were soon snapped off by a vigorous wave. Distraught, she cried tears no larger than the tiny baubles.

Terry Fitzgerald, a young man who'd competed in the event, surfaced at her side.

"What's wrong, my love?" His curly hair was like an off-shore breeze on glassy water.

"I lost my pearl necklace."

"There now. It's back with Mother Ocean."

"You think?"

"I know." As Terry made a date with Pandra they were captured on camera by Dane Flashman, making a surfing film. They were also watched, from the debris-crowded shore, by Tracy Mixx, who'd seen her at Homecoming and in the town Pandra was already starting to erase.

Later, farther south, Debbie dispatched Pandra to Taco Bell while she herself waited at the Sunset Smoothie Shop. "Quick!" she said. "Destroy the bags! We can't be seen eating Taco Bell!" Pandra transferred the food, in its orange-soaked wrappers, into a sand-colored bag. The coconut-papaya smoothies came in styrofoam tubs.

"All right, Pandra!" Debbie said. "A date with a celebrity! Are you stoked?"

Pandra, never one for vernacular, just looked down.

Their date, to a surfing film, impressed Pandra only because she was able to get in for free. In fact, it turned out to be not a date at all—Terry Fitzgerald had been called away to the North Shore and had left word with an indifferent Pandra that she should simply mention his name at the box office.

Pandra went alone to the movie that night, savoring the power of being solo. The crowd's catcalls were for rounded waves and hollow tubes, and occasionally for toasted girls with long-blond-hair-parted-in-the-middle. The soundtrack—Hendrix, Steve Miller, John Mayall, HONK—seemed to spur the waves on.

On the way to her car (parked as far as possible from Jack's Surf Shop, as the vehicle was an unfashionable, city-daubed Nova without surf racks even), she spotted a blue VW Bug with regulation racks. Pandra knew Debbie would okay it; vans and gunboats should never have racks—that would be showing off, since boards would fit easily inside.

"Wait up," Pandra heard; she kept walking.

"No, please, wait." She didn't stop, but glanced over her shoulder and saw Tracy. He caught up and placed an abalone shell in her hand. Nestled in it was a luminous necklace of pukka shells, taut and smooth.

"I heard about what happened and wanted to make it up to you."

Pandra thought he was referring to the fact that she'd been stood up.

"I'm sorry, but I couldn't afford pearls."

Pandra knew then what he meant, and felt touched, a light undertow.

"Thanks," she said. Tracy walked Pandra the rest of the way to her car.

The next day in class, while attempting to pair chromosomes, Pandra told Debbie about Tracy.

"But where's he from?" Debbie asked.

"I don't know. Newport, I think."

"As long as he's not from inland."

"No, I don't think so," Pandra said, as unsure now of her potential match as she was of the x's and y's she'd hypothesized on paper.

Debbie said nothing more, but worried about what this meant to her cherished friendship with Pandra. In her mind, she saw Pandra no longer riding over on her 10-speed after school to look at clothes, to talk and laugh, to make fake telephone calls. Debbie saw herself minus a beach partner, eating lunch alone. That upcoming summer Pandra wouldn't be there to cheer her on, from her place on the narrow sidewalk of Disneyland's Main Street, as Debbie toddled along in the Electrical Parade. Pandra wouldn't run wild with her, making mischief within the heavily controlled confines of the theme park.

Then Debbie thought of her brother, Tom, who was quickly advancing within the Disney organization: one minute he was serving ice cream, the next he was an Imagineer, making plans for Disney World. Debbie knew Pandra idolized Tom, and wouldn't forsake her connection with him. She felt reassured as she pictured Pandra sitting cross-legged on her brother's floor, watching screenings of *Meet Me in Saint Louis* on his then-very-rare videotape machine.

She saw Pandra gazing into his stained-glass fish tank and standing awestruck next to the hourglass from *The Wizard of Oz*, which Tom had purchased at the 1970 MGM auction.

Later that school day, Debbie would step into a dress picked up at that same auction, where dozens of starlet costumes and gowns from musicals were sold under junk-shop circumstances. Busby Berkeley chorus-line dresses fanned the floors as buyers kicked them aside, snapping up treasures at dime-store prices.

Having received a special reprieve from such physical education activities as swimming and basketball, Debbie found no way out of taking the even more embarrassing square-dancing unit. Today was the day of her final, and she needed the credit to pass, to leave school behind forever. So she placed special emphasis on her costume, even vowing to be civil to her partner, who was being bused in from another school.

The visiting students from Marineland High found the inland air stifling; they labored to show the effort of breathing. They also protested the smog and the way it coated their hair, destroying its windblown possibilities. Thus, sullenly, they filed into the auditorium and squared off.

As Debbie honored her partner, she smiled a kind of sneer. Then, curtsying to her corner, her heart surged like her MGM petticoats.

The boy, named Mack, had algae-green eyes and brown hair that put him at odds with his surfer buddies, as did his oil-industry family. But Debbie neither knew nor considered this aspect of Mack as she sashayed left, then circled to the right. By the time she and Mack do-si-do'd, she visualized herself answering "I do." At the first promenade, the group cascaded around the gym; by the time the ladies led, Debbie had an idea. She'd promenade her corner right out the exit door.

As she did, she wasn't alone. The entire combined class followed her through the double doors and were now at large and unruly on the blacktop, around the track, and all over the far hockey field.

When Debbie was given triple detentions and threatened with suspension, she only smiled.

Pandra heard about Debbie's exploits while she was scribbling in yearbook class, an extension of journalism her advisor had nudged her into. At present her classmates were readying captions for Senior Ditch Day. Jim, the class photographer, heard about the free-for-all on the field and rushed out, grabbing Pandra as his reporter.

"Don't pull me!" Pandra bit, because she thought she should.

Jim said, "I'm sorry. I'm just excited."

"Oh, it's okay," Pandra conceded. "It's just graduation jitters, I guess."

"Sure. Right, whatever you say. Everyone knows you and Debbie think you're too good for us inlanders."

Pandra considered this, but didn't answer. Instead, the Homecoming Queen in her did. "It's just an act, Jimbo. We're kind of afraid of you guys, you know—the brains, or the sportos even. We think you'd reject us."

"You should try and find out," Jim replied as they hurried past the auditorium, almost trampling the senior-class tree. They arrived at the field, which looked like a free festival with Mr. Hurley, the principal, as MC.

"Line up now!" he barked through the foghorn. "Those who don't, won't graduate!" And little by little the students came back, lining up in vaguely alphabetical order. Jim snapped action photos, paparazzi-style, as Pandra looked around for Debbie.

No one told Pandra her sidekick was cooling her grass-stained tennies in the office, but someone did tell Jim, who relayed it to Pandra.

"Maybe I'd better go there," Pandra said.

"Only if you've got a thing for detention, too," Jim warned. "Mr. Hurley seems pretty pissed."

Once Jim talked Pandra out of it, she got the sense he was trying to ask her out. "I know what you're doing," she said, "and I think it's really sweet. Only I'm kind of seeing some-one."

"I'll bet he's a peroxide-head," Jim answered, unwittingly mimicking Debbie's lingo. "And I'll just bet he's from the beach."

"His hair's naturally bleached out, and he's from New-port."

"Does he compete?"

"Compete? You mean in surf meets? No, I don't think so. I think he just surfs to be close to nature."

"Yeah, right," laughed Jim. "Mother Ocean and all that shit."

"He's not like that," Pandra defended as their teacher, Mrs. Brown, came up to their double desk.

"What are you two up to?" she asked.

"We've been having a field day," Jim said. "Only Princess Pandra here probably won't admit it."

"Pandra?" Mrs. Brown questioned.

"We just went out to the field so Jim could get some pic-tures."

"Jim, I think the yearbook has enough pictures of Pandra by now."

"What?" Pandra asked, incredulous. "No, not of me. Of the kids."

"Did you show Pandra yet?" Mrs. Brown asked Jim.

"We've, um, kind of made a two-page spread out of your story. Homecoming and all that," Jim revealed.

What?" Pandra demanded, trying to hide how thrilled she was. "You can't do that! I'll look like a goon, a geek!"

"Now, be a sport, Pandra," Mrs. Brown warned. "One day you can show it to your grandchildren."

"I'm not going to have any grandchildren! I'm going to live alone in a cliff house overlooking the Big Sur coastline. I'm going to have a piano and a typewriter—and a cat!"

Jim laughed. "Does Joni Mitchell know about this? She'll be pretty worried."

"Oh, shut up!"

"Haven't you seen *Play Misty for Me?*" Jim goaded.

"Jim, be quiet now," Mrs. Brown advised. "Pandra deserves her dreams. In fact, she'll probably get them."

After the first of her detentions, Debbie called Pandra at home. Pandra got up from the dinner table.

"What happened?" she asked. "Can I come over?"

"Nah, I'll see you at school tomorrow. And what's happened, Pandy, is that I'm in love."

The day Pandra herself knew she was in love, she was in American History class. The teacher was lecturing about Herbert Hoover and the Return to Normalcy. Her text, its uncracked spine finishing-school straight, stressed that "normalcy" was not a real word, and that Hoover was the first president to create a lexicon of his own for the mass media.

Pandra's high-school days were overseen by President Nixon, but she bothered little with politics, except so far as they concerned coastal access. Still, the word "normalcy" stuck in her mind, and she carried it forward, as she'd done in basic math, to the poetry period that came next.

The day's verse assignment was to bring in song lyrics. Pandra was pretty much indifferent to pop music, except for Joni Mitchell and Neil Young. But two songs from her childhood stuck like that "normalcy": "I Will Follow Him" and "Walking in the Sand."

When Pandra read aloud the lyrics to the former, Little Peggy March's tantrum no longer seemed antifeminist. In Pandra's dispassionate monotone it was an irreverent statement, and she intended the irony.

From his seat behind her, Jim listened, awed.

"Pandra," Jim called after class. "Wait up. That, what you read, was really righteous."

"Thanks."

"How's Newport?"

"I haven't been lately."

"You know what I mean," Jim sighed.

"I don't know! Listen, I have to go and find Debbie. She wasn't in homeroom."

"I think I saw her name on the absence report."

"Bummer." Pandra stopped in the quad before turning to go back towards her locker.

Jim shuffled in his Wallaby shoes. "Are you planning on going to the prom, or is that too rah-rah for you?"

"I haven't really thought about it." Pandra stopped short of adding *Why?*

"Catch you later." Jim ran off, having spied a friend, and

Pandra advanced to her locker, thinking about the next poetry assignment: finding art in an advertisement.

"Burma-shave?" Pandra's mom suggested, trying to be helpful.

Pandra had very few sheltered bays in her life but Tracy Mixx promised to be one. Talking on the phone, they felt that all others were interlopers in their paradise. One of their dates was at the Balboa Theater in Newport, to see a movie called *Pacific Vibrations*. When Pandra glimpsed a crowd scene she knew she'd featured prominently in, she dropped her purse at the opportune moment, for Tracy to pick up.

Audrey warned Pandra not to toy with Tracy as she had her other school admirers, projecting onto her daughter her own regrets at having married a man who lived for something unspecified, something an arm's length out of his grasp.

Although it was spring, Pandra considered her time with Tracy as a summer of love.

At PE class the day after the movie, she left the pukka shells he'd given her with some other jewelry in her locker, which she failed to secure: locking up was time-consuming and viewed by the other girls as paranoid. Besides, gym was for rushing through, for taking shy showers in your bra and underwear. When Pandra returned from running the track, the shells were gone, along with a metronome charm and a turquoise ring that her grandmother had been given by a Mandan Indian boyfriend back in 1915. Pandra mourned these losses, puzzling why only the metronome had been pried from her charm bracelet.

Heading on to her poetry class, where she would present her art-in-advertising assignment, she wished Debbie were in school that day and not away with her brother in Florida.

Through a haze of distress, she managed to say, "My ad's one for Joni Mitchell's album, *Ladies of the Canyon*. It's about this girl who lives in Laurel Canyon and a grocery boy who delivers some stuff. It's about the sunset and the record she listens to, to keep her company. There's a drawing too, but really it's more like a story than an ad."

"Could you read some of it to us?" Mrs. Brown asked.

At the close of the reading, she said, "I think this is really about the way Joni Mitchell's fans want to live: alone, independent, adventurous—and not in the city."

"That's great," Mrs. Brown said and Pandra felt more relaxed. From the next desk, Jim smiled.

While she went out with Tracy, Pandra still wore training bras, undetectable under huge jersey dresses loose at her tiny waist, itself a mere monocle. She favored chintz crisscross shoes with wedged rubber rickrack soles—$2.99 a pair at Woolworth's, available in red, blue or a floral print.

The shoes were a cushion of comfort for her as much as her periods were a source of pain. Days before they were due, she would wear pads pinned to her bikini bottoms, at the beach even, where they became waterlogged and dragged heavily beneath her. Pandra didn't wear tampons and was afraid of any sort of penetration. Her doctor counseled her about this and suggested it was a fear of intimacy, a phobia of loss. She once tried to insert a Tampax and cried in confusion, having to ask Debbie to help her take it out.

Pandra's mother was too ill now to talk to her daughter about such things. She was wasting away to a small, conical shell. It was, however, Pandra's father who died first, from the grief. At his funeral, Pandra remembered how, during the first moon landing and walk, she and her father had gone out to the 7-11 store, driving down streets as listless as the moon's surface, to buy more whiskey. The clerk never looked at the father and daughter; his eyes were fixed on the inscrutable TV screen.

The day after her father's funeral, Pandra returned to school, where Debbie approached her without her usual bravado. "Are you okay?" she asked.

"I got to ride in a limo," Pandra replied.

In yearbook class, Jim was equally cautious. "If this isn't a good time, let me know," he ventured, "but I wanted to ask you something again."

Pandra was wearing a cape, sewn out of a sari-like bedspread. She wouldn't remove it, even though the school air-conditioning was malfunctioning. "Sure, what is it?"

"Were you planning on going to the prom? Or is it uncool? I don't mean to be snotty, I was just wondering."

"I'm going with Tracy to Harbor's prom, and ours, too."

"Righteous," Jim replied. "Well, I was wondering too if you're okay."

"Yeah, I'm bitchin'," Pandra said, feeling suddenly self-conscious because she never comfortably used slang, which she believed only pointed up her inappropriateness. She felt it exposed her for the fraud she was, a scared little girl trying to act superior to her classmates, almost any of whom she would have traded places with.

Later that afternoon, fetching a towel from the back of Tracy's car, Pandra found a cube of a new kind of surf wax, alluringly called Sex Wax. She unwrapped it and sniffed it. Then she kept the wrapper, a souvenir.

Pandra walked the long, narrow San Onofre shore to Trestles, where Tracy rode on a southwest swell. Placing herself on the sand more or less in line with him in the water, she saw Tracy suddenly angle away on a nice right. An hour later he put his board down next to where Pandra had fallen asleep. He straddled the board's fiberglass shape. A blond teenager approached slowly, wobbling in the difficult sand as Pandra stirred awake. The boy struggled to carry a twin-finned kneeboard.

"Tracy, my man," he said. He gently put his board down in order to extend his only arm. "Fucking chemotherapy, man. I just couldn't stay out. Plus, my paddling's not worth shit."

"Dave, this is Pandra," Tracy said.

"Hi. I'm heading home," Dave explained. "I only stopped for a second, to catch my breath. Have you been south much?"

"I keep meaning to go to Puerto but I'm waiting for a hurricane," Tracy said. "Listen, do you want some help walking back to the lot?"

"No way. Catch you later."

"Take care, man."

Tracy and Pandra watched Dave walk southward. Just before slipping out of sight, he climbed aboard a lifeguard's yellow jeep.

Tracy said, "Dave used to surf down by the nuclear-power plant. He claimed the waves were better and the water was warmer."

Pandra didn't reply. When Tracy dropped her at her home, he kissed her good-bye and she was like a dummy, deflated of emotion, devoid of a desire to fight for a life that seemed cornered by death. In her room that night, she heard her father's remembered voice. She got up to look for him on the back porch, in the yellow moth-deflecting hue, bathed in a permanent half-light.

On Sunday, she and Tracy went to the finals at the South Street surf meet in curio-cute Laguna Beach. "Are you sure you want to go?" Pandra had questioned. "Competitiveness just seems so mean."

"It's a way to see the masters in action," Tracy responded. "Besides, afterwards we can hit the Crab Cooker for a meal. A treat for my wahine."

South Street was steep and Pandra and Tracy stood at its high point, holding the railing of a stairway to the beach, craning for a view of the contest. Pandra was bored but lacked the voice to say so.

Over clam chowder and fish on disposable dishes, she cleared her throat to speak. "Tracy, are you going to come with me to my prom?"

"Sure, babe," he said. "I'm still thinking about the contest. It was awesome, huh? Terry Fitzgerald is just righteous."

"For sure," said Pandra, thinking of her bedroom walls covered with the Australian's corkscrew-haired visage, his eyes the color of *Surfer* magazine water, and remembering too their encounter at the River Jetty. "I wish he didn't compete, though."

"He has to. He's the best. He also does it to get money so he can keep surfing. And endorsements and stuff like that—that way he doesn't have to work a job. He's free to just ride the waves."

"I can't get into the meets. They're like a circus. It's almost as sickening as the whole 'locals only' thing, that territorial nonsense. So LA."

"I don't know about that. There's not many beaches in LA

we'd want."

"No," said Pandra. "I didn't mean it like that. I meant the mentality was so LA."

"My genius girlfriend," Tracy laughed. "Talking about head trips like they mean something."

When Pandra got home that evening, her mother had left her a note: *Debbie called.* Nothing more. Audrey had gone to bed but Pandra could hear music from her sister's room.

She knocked on the door. "Can I come in ?"

She found Ellen studying a college textbook.

"You know, Pandra, you could stay home and keep mom company once in a while. It wouldn't kill you."

"Oh, come on! I do."

"No, you don't. You're either with Tracy or on the phone with Debbie, or just out of it in your room. Anyway, what is it?"

"Do you know what time Debbie phoned?"

"No, and I don't care."

"Okay!" Pandra left.

Ellen had her own phone line; the princess phone glowed on her crowded desk. She hadn't given out her unlisted number yet, planning to wait until after finals. It rang now, an unfamiliar sound. Pandra listened at Ellen's door.

"Hello? Hello? Wait! Pandra?"

From her place outside the door, Pandra scurried back to her own room, and then again down the short hall. "Yeah?"

"That was really weird," her sister said. "When the phone rang, the receiver kind of leaped off its cradle. I picked it up and a voice said 'This is Mrs. Elliott from down the road. Tell your mother I'll be seeing her in a few days.'"

Pandra and Ellen stared at each other. Mrs. Elliott had

died in a car crash several years before.

That night Pandra slept in her sister's trundle bed. When she got home from school Monday afternoon, her mother had been admitted to the hospital. Pandra waited for Ellen to get home from college so they could drive there. On the way to the hospital, Pandra told her sister, "Debbie told me she's moving to Oklahoma with her boyfriend. I don't know what I'm going to do!" She cried and was still in tears when she reached her mother's bedside, where her grandmother waited.

"I'm afraid this is it," the old woman said flatly.

That night, Audrey Jane died. Pandra and Ellen, orphaned now, let the dirty dishes pile up and the dust thicken. They had to push hard on the bathroom door to shift the growing mountain of soiled laundry on the other side.

On the morning of Pandra's prom day, Tracy called collect. "I'm taking off for a few days," he said. "There's a hurricane off Baja, major juice."

Pandra didn't remind him it was her prom night. She stayed in and watched TV, while Ellen went out on a date. When Tracy came back from Mexico, he brought her drop earrings made of abalone.

They were alone at Pandra's house. Tracy cooed and kissed her, but she moved away. "I have no feeling for you," she explained. "I have no feeling for anything."

"Maybe we should cool it for a while," he suggested. "A gang of us were going to go to Big Surf anyway. There's this joke surf meet, but the prize money's good."

Big Surf was a concrete wave machine in Tempe, Arizona. Pandra was speechless at first. "You might as well just keep on going," she said then. "I can't believe you're going to compete."

"What's with the gnarly behavior? Are you on the rag again or something?" Tracy stormed out with the velocity of a Baja weather inversion.

At graduation, Debbie and Pandra were reprimanded for wearing floral muumuus under their white robes. This would go on their permanent records, they were told. When Pandra got home that night, she found an envelope taped to her door. Inside was a note, and a charm: half a heart with a jagged edge.

Dear Pandra, Sorry I didn't make graduation. I'm off for Seattle, where I'm going to college, starting with summer school. I wish we could have worked out, had a try even.
And I hope life gives you all you dream of. It's already won you my heart. Jim

Before she fell asleep that night, the transistor radio beneath her pillow, she heard the song "The End of the World." And she felt it really was.

Tracy sent her a postcard of nondescript London Bridge, the monolith anomaly in the Arizona desert. Pandra threw the card at the overstuffed kitchen trashcan.

Pandra started to have sleep-delaying nights, the solace of a symmetrical eight hours distorted into an infinity of denial. She took to sitting up and watching TV, hearing the canned sound of horses' hooves as she started to drop off, then waking to the loll of Gene Autry's silent-siren guitar.

The days of summer vacation gaped ahead. Debbie was packing her things and Pandra still went to the beach, only to become restless once she got there. Even the waves seemed to reject her and spit her out, so out of kilter was she with their bitter timing.

She offered to drive Debbie to the airport, as her family refused to help their daughter in her impetuous decision. Pandra thought of her own mom and how she would marvel at the presence of seagulls in their neighborhood, looking so out of place in the supermarket parking lot.

The gray of the sky permeated the landscape as Pandra set off for the airport with Debbie. She said good-bye outside the terminal, hoping to shorten, if not lessen, the pain.

"I promise I'll write," Debbie swore; Pandra was bemused, a light relief to her grief. Debbie never even had a pen, let alone paper.

"Love you to death," Debbie exclaimed and crushed Pandra in a thin-framed hug.

"Me too." Pandra didn't watch Debbie pass out of sight; she feared she'd never see her again.

On the way home, Pandra decided to take a detour; she drove down Sunset Boulevard from its pristine Westwood end to the more disheveled downtown. Somewhere in the middle, next to Famous Amos Cookies, she pulled to the side, her eyes stinging from smoggy rain.

At curb level, she saw a silver platform boot stacked like the nearby Capitol Records building. As she looked up, following the boot, she saw a boy whose hair both stood at and demanded attention. A feather boa wrapped his neck like an overzealous lover, and his souvenir T-shirt rode up his midriff like a flag ascending a pole. His cuffed pants, too, were hiked up, the better to display the city skyline painted on the boots. The girl with him paled by comparison, though she was hardly drab—like the top and middle of a traffic signal, her crisscross top was fire-engine red, while her neon satin shorts were the color of caution.

"Glitter people," Pandra murmured before starting up to head back to Orange County by the inland route.

Shortly after Tracy had disappeared from Pandra's summer life, he vanished altogether. Rumors cropped up that he had a pregnant girlfriend in Mexico. Pandra closed her ears to this. For her, he'd died once he decided to compete in that exaggeratedly artificial surf match.

That was what she said, anyway. In truth, she had felt stranded ever since he'd proved unwilling and unable to console her after she'd lost her parents. Pandra thought he could have gone a short way, at least, to make up for the gap she felt. But he never even tried.

So she blamed his "plastic-ness," his artifice—even as such a veneer began to hold a very great allure for her. She began to do incongruous things, like wearing a T-shirt boasting *Hollywood* over her bark-cloth bikini. She fantasized seeing her name in the same block capitals as that tattered sign.

One day Pandra drove back from the beach alone, along a stretch of El Toro Road. The military base on her right was about to become the landing strip for Air Force One, carrying Richard Nixon for the last time. When the plane touched ground, Nixon would no longer be president. Pandra heard an aircraft overhead and vaguely reflected—politics were pretty much a back lot in her life. She was aware of its markers, of course: the public deaths, the dinnertime war, but her engagement with them was limited to having worn a black armband in the school quad on Vietnam Moratorium Day in 1970. At that time, she was too blameless even to draw detention. Debbie, not yet her friend, had probably just ditched and gone shopping.

Just this morning she'd received a letter from Debbie, telling about her job in a clothing shop in Tulsa, where she'd waited on most of Leon Russell's Shelter People, notably Eric Clapton, who, Debbie claimed, had a 24-inch waist. Patti Harrison was "curt," Merry Clayton "dowdy." Debbie herself was fine, enamored of clogs made by Olaf Daughters, sandals by Bare Traps, and jeans by Sisley. She'd done a bit of showroom modeling and had a new friend who'd been featured in *Mademoiselle.*

Come visit, Pandy, you'll love it, she'd written, putting a heart in place of the word love. And she signed off, *I love you,* the word "love" bloated, the ink running together.

Pandra smiled. She'd never been on a plane, she realized, as Air Force One glided into view. It might take some doing to get her to Oklahoma.

When Pandra arrived home, some photographs her sister had taken were lying on the dining-room table. There were shots of Pandra skateboarding six months earlier, mixed in with pictures of her parents—as if that were normal, as if they were still around.

Pandra had started to think of her mother and father as film stars. Her mom was Bette Davis in *Dark Victory;* her father was harder to pin down. She looked at their faces in the shiny photos, then moaned when she came to her own image. She looked haggard, as if her face and clothes alike were outworn and faded. She saw she lacked the glamour of her mother at the same age, as well as her spirit and quiet strength.

Maybe she should buy red lipstick, Pandra thought. The last time she'd worn makeup, it had been Yardley's cake eyeliner, which had transferred promptly from her lids to the heights of her arched eyebrows.

With her sister busy at summer school and working part-time in a department store, Pandra began to weary of Orange County. It felt like starched clothes, unwelcome on her still-forming body.

She needed a job before she started college. Still, the idea of slaving away in the intolerable county was like drudgery piled onto boredom. If she must work, she decided, it would have to be in Los Angeles, where there was an energy Pandra would have described as "negative" three months ago.

She began to peruse the *Los Angeles Times* classifieds—tiny compared to the *View* section full of gossip she'd previously limited herself to. The day she was to register at a community college on the Los Angeles/Orange County border, she drove a little farther north, back to the middle of Sunset Boulevard. She parked next to the Preview House, which test-marketed television shows and commercials on a random and eager audience. Pandra crossed the street and entered a low-slung building, nondescript in comparison to the clam-on-the-halfshell Preview House.

When she exited, it was with a different gait, for she was now an Amber Girl, about to work for a telephone-answering service three days a week. The rest of the time, she guessed, she was still Pandra, a girl who bore as much relation to her high-school self as the cover photos of teach-yourself-guitar books usually did to their users.

Pandra walked a short block to All-American Burger, where she recognized Flo and Eddie, of the benign '60s pop group the Turtles. The duo now hosted a wicked rock-and-roll comedy show on underground radio. She picked up her iced tea and fries from the sliding glass service window and sat at a plastic table near the pair, happy to be lunching with celebrities now.

A few days later, early on Saturday evening, Pandra felt not quite here or there. It was still too early to go out, assuming Pandra had somewhere to go, which she didn't. Nor did she have the clothes.

Ellen, also at loose ends, suggested they go to a thrift store in an adjoining neighborhood. Pandra thought her sister must be mistaken: nothing was open on Saturday night, not even South Coast Plaza.

"Sears is," Ellen responded with a laugh. "Remember how you used to like to go there and get those chocolate stars? And nonpareils! You called them non-parallels."

"Well, they were circle-shaped!" Pandra defended. It was a poignant recollection, even though the time it evoked was no more than three months ago.

Ellen went to get ready. By now she'd moved unselfconsciously into their parents' room. While Pandra waited, she switched on the TV. Where there was once *Boss City*, a '60s stomp, there was now *The Real Don Steele Show*, which played mostly unhip music, often by an in-studio outfit called the Carpenters (with the oddity of a girl drummer). Still, the show drew a number of Hollywood types, glitter-and-glam groupies who often plastered the pages of *Star* magazine and crowded the tiny floor of Rodney's English Disco on the Sunset Strip. And vamping it up to "Jet," by Paul McCartney and Wings, was the boy with the feather boa and the tall shoes, swaying and starring in front of the girl Pandra had seen with him that day in the rain.

The fast-shouting deejay shook his short Prince Valiant haircut and peered out from his pink-lensed aviator glasses.

"Ohhh! Names, names!" he demanded of the duo.

"Chuckie," sighed the boy.

"Mona," gum-popped his girl in a wildly fake English accent.

The show's host pulled another couple, two girls, out of what was transforming into an impromptu limbo line. "Topaz," said the one in a dress studded with rhinestones over star patterns. "Lana Lamé," exclaimed a dizzy blonde, swaying on stacked heels that contrasted with her flat chest bearhugged by a tiny T-shirt.

Pandra was transported by their shiny clothes, metallic threads vibrating through them like electric currents. She looked down at her own drabness: a faded and bled Guatemalan blouse, its lapsed elastic neckline drooping off her shoulders and under her fine arms. She began to imagine all she'd buy: a leopard-print handbag, shoes with cigarette-holder heels by Frederick's of Hollywood, satin halter tops, rhinestone jackets. Platform tennis shoes, Hot Socks snarling under shoe tongues. Seamed hose. Exaggerated dark glasses so she'd never have to look at the sun again.

At the thrift store, Pandra succeeded in picking up some of these items, spending uncharted time in the lingerie section. Her mother had always forbidden her to buy underwear, nightclothes, and shoes secondhand. In the kids' section, she found a tiny tourist shirt boasting *New York City* in skywriting over several landmarks.

Ellen watched her sister's supermarket cart fill up with treasures. She welcomed the change, however abrupt, from Pandra's recent lifelessness.

"Why can't I find any platforms?" Pandra asked.

"You'll probably have to buy new ones. They haven't been

around long enough to end up here."

"But Grandma mentioned that Carmen Miranda used to wear them."

"Maybe. But Carmen Miranda probably doesn't live in Santa Ana."

"Is she still alive?"

"I don't know," Ellen shrugged. "Still, you should get new ones. I don't think worn-out platforms would have the same effect."

"You know, you're right. Take a good look," said Pandra, doing a twirl. "This is the last of the frumpy me."

The two sisters raced their carts to the checkout, Pandra winning in a photo finish.

At home, the late concert on TV had been postponed, and screening instead was a repeat of David Bowie's *1980 Floor Show*. The performer, half Martian, half marionette, sang one song as plastic disembodied hands hugged him, provoking a nervous, sexual giggle in Pandra. "Artifice for art's sake," her sister swiped, before going off to bed. "I'll stick with George Orwell myself."

Pandra wasn't sure what Ellen meant but she thought it sounded good—sophisticated, even.

Between acts, including Marianne Faithfull dressed as a nun, there were commercials touting David Bowie's new LP, *Pin-Ups*. His made-up face looked like a sideshow cutout, as if he'd put his own face inside a larger, garish one and, after being warned repeatedly not to do that, got stuck there. The picture rang true for Pandra; she thought of her own moldy makeup tray, her mirror speckled with flecks of whiteheads and toothpaste.

She'd buy this record, she knew, just as she once bought

and discarded the fall issue of *Seventeen*, but this time she'd learn to put her makeup on by it. The cover was eerily familiar, too: Bowie's pallor and emaciated cheeks were so much like her mother's, near the end. When Pandra went to bed that night, she felt comfortable in the sheets; they reassured and supported her like test-driven wings.

Sunday night, just before she was to begin as an Amber Girl, Pandra and Ellen went to see Stephen Stills and Manassas at the UFO-domed Anaheim Convention Center, a street and two parking lots away from Disneyland. In the darkened sports arena, musicians clotted the makeshift stage. To Pandra they looked as dated as postcards of beaches or freeways, depicting tanned bodies or shark-finned cars.

When the dishwater-blond singer launched into his current signature song, "Love the One You're With," Pandra felt slicked by the unwelcome gaze of the guy seated beside her, who looked redundant in a faded lumberjack shirt and high-waisted jeans. As Stills sang, "There's a girl right next to you/ and she's just waiting for something to do," the boy tilted a fine-pencil joint in Pandra's direction.

She refused, almost politely, and vowed to herself (the kind of zealous promise that had the greatest chance of being kept) that she'd wear her glitter clothes at all times now, to all events. Their inherent glare would ward off this kind of intrusion.

Driving to work the next day, Pandra listened to KCAT-FM. She learned that the girl with Bowie on the *Pin-Ups* cover was Twiggy. Well, thought Pandra, if a '60s icon can mutate that successfully, even at her age, then so can I. She squirmed as she drove, a spectacle in her secondhand girl-group glitter top, which walled her torso far less safely than the seat belt did.

She thought again of the glitter couple, how she'd seen them in person in the rain. She consigned the memory to the part of her mind reserved for things to come back to over and over.

Her job involved sitting in a tiny cubicle paneled streaky brown, using a phone headset that made her look as if she were commanding an antiquated space mission. She sat, with carbon-leafed spiral notebook, leaky Bic pen at the ready to take down whatever messages came in for her seemingly important or tragically hopeful clients. And the calls did come, generally from sullen voices resentful to be speaking to her, an interloper in their scheme of immediacy. Pandra waited and spoke, crossed and uncrossed her legs, and generally counted the minutes until her breaks.

As the inflated gloved hand on her Mickey Mouse watch pointed choosily toward Pandra's chest, she fairly leaped up, pushed her chair into the bay of her desk, and exited for the All-American Burger. She ordered her lunch and then sat outside at a table bordering the moderate midday traffic of central Sunset Boulevard. Kitty-corner to her, monopolizing a table for four, was a bottle blonde: a one-bottle blonde, that is, for this girl seemed to have shunned the toner entirely. She wore cuffed jeans, a stripy top, and a cropped velvet blazer trimmed by a star-and-comet rhinestone pin.

Pandra recognized the girl from TV, and found herself storing up the courage to say something. Suddenly the blonde spoke.

"Are you going to use that ketchup, or is it just there to decorate your table?"

It took Pandra a moment to realize she was being addressed.

"No, no. I don't use ketchup," she replied haltingly.

"Well, sling it over here, then," the girl commanded in a West Coast version of screwball Brooklynese. "Bring yourself over, too, if you can find room."

Pandra collected her burger in its styrofoam nest, gathered stray fries in a napkin. She made a second trip for her drink and lastly, for the ketchup, sticky in its red plastic applicator.

"Such a buildup." The girl laughed at Pandra's labors. "I'm Lana, by the way. But you can call me Lana Lamé."

"Hi. I'm Pandra."

"Did you make that up?"

"No, my parents. I think it was a tribute name, a combination of things. I never found out what they were."

"I like you," Lana conceded.

"Thanks. Do you live around here?"

"Ha! The hills aren't the only thing that are steep. No, this is a lit-tle out of my price range. I live in the Valley but I work here, at P-U House."

"Where?"

"Preview House. That's my name for it, because it stinks."

"Oh, that's right next to me. I'm an Amber Girl!"

"What the hell's that supposed to be?" Lana made a face on her burger with squirts of ketchup.

"It's supposed to be an answering service."

"Oh. Do you get paid okay?"

"Three-fifty an hour."

"Not that great," Lana pronounced. "I'm at five bucks, barely. But it's bull-pucky work, filling in these forms that people have already filled in, I mean putting their answers into categories and all that." Lana paused, frustrated. "I can't really explain it too good, but a monkey could do it and be a lot nicer to work with."

"You mean your co-workers?"

"Straight jerk-offs. They hate me and I hate them."

"I guess I'm lucky in that," Pandra said. "No one sees us, so we can wear what we want."

"Oh, no, it's not that. I can pretty much wear anything if I can put up with their stares. That's what's the pits."

"Well, I think you look great," Pandra ventured.

"Thanks. You look okay yourself, but you could use a haircut."

Pandra touched her hair, unchanged since cheerleading days.

"You should get a Ziggy cut, a shag." Lana's own hair was Jean Harlow's without the luster.

"I've thought about it," Pandra lied.

"My friend Topaz cuts hair at the Back Street store," Lana continued, suddenly affecting a Southern drawl. "But she's limited to doing shit like blue rinses. Not radical blue rinses either. I'm talking little old lady from Pasadena. But sometimes she sees people at her home, in San Gabriel, and does their hair there." Lana stopped for a moment. "Do you want me to ask her?"

"Sure," said Pandra, suddenly exalted.

Topaz lived above a garage in a Spanish-style single apartment. The mock adobe was mildewed inside and out. The alley that trimmed her front window carried on to the San Gabriel Mission, where it skirted the graveyard. Outside, Pandra used a doorknocker so gently it sounded like a timid woodpecker. When there was no response, she wondered if Lana had given her the right directions. Suddenly Topaz, filament-bright, opened the creaky door. Strewn behind her on the bed like inverted question marks were several bent coat hangers, pants, an ostrich boa, and a six-foot fringed scarf. Topaz glided in her four-inch wedged shoes, as nonchalantly as if she were barefoot.

Pandra looked not at Topaz but at her steamer-trunk-cum-coffee-table, dotted not with travel stickers but an array of *Star* magazines and the considerably less glossy *Free Press*.

"Hey, I'm Topaz," the girl said, offering Pandra the mood ring on her index finger as if she were a kind of Pope. "What's your name again? Sorry... Lana Lamé told me, but it's gone and slipped my mind."

"Pandra."

"Cor."

Pandra kept eyeing the bed, as if it were set up for some ghastly experiment. She wondered why Topaz put on a mock Cockney accent that fit her throat like a cowl-necked sweater and probably slipped just as often.

Topaz smoothed her high-waisted Sisley jeans with pearl snaps on each hip pocket. Their belled reaches were a curtain rising over her Fred Slatten shoes, hand-painted to depict the Manhattan skyline.

"I like your pants," Pandra said, for want of anything else.

"Thanks, luv. I've got two new pairs over on the bed. Here, let me show you these." Quick as a confident wink, Topaz slid gracefully out of her jeans. She staggered only slightly as she didn't take off her shoes and stepped into a satin pair of Dittos. She then fell flat back on her bed, flailing her legs in the air, a victory sign. She pulled the pants over heel and calf. "Here's where you come in," she told Pandra. "Grab the coat hanger."

Pandra did so.

"Now put the hook in the zipper and yank!" Topaz lifted her bottom off the bed, an overturned scarab, and Pandra plied the zipper with the hanger. Topaz squawked and it took several tries. The Dittos were so tight they were superfluous; the basest coat of paint.

"They look good," Pandra attested. She herself had never been that shameless, thinking of her own pink ski pants, in a '60s bad-girl style, which would have been naughty now only for the girl next door.

"Now to get them off," Topaz announced, pulling at the waistband like a film of cellophane. "You can't expect me to do your hair in them."

"So," she said eventually. "What are we going to do about this mop?"

Pandra resisted speaking. Topaz's own hair—a nondescript fawny brown—was the single unremarkable feature about her.

"I know what you're thinking," Topaz chirped. "That I've got a lot of nerve." She vigorously chomped several pieces of bubble gum. "Well, a lot you know. See, my hair is naturally blond, white blond with a few strands of yellow-gold. So what do I do? I dye it brown. The way I see it, that's about as outrageous as you can get: a blond who goes brown." Topaz moved a few feet away to fetch scissors from a skirted dressing table far more primly clad than she.

Watching her flourish the scissors, Pandra noticed Topaz's nails, painted with tiny black slits, like cats' eyes in direct sunlight. "I don't know about those pants," Topaz said. "I feel like I grow out of them just by exhaling!" And she laughed, a lot, at her own joke.

"Lana Lamé said something like I should get a Ziggy cut."

"Not right for you," Topaz snapped, quickly for once. "No. I saw a girl at Rodney's the other night—have you ever been? No, I suppose not. Anyway she had a platinum swirl kind of like, I don't know, Betty Grable or someone. Probably her, yeah, because she's called Betty Able. So if I did that with a dash of Angie, you'd be fab."

"You think?"

"Don't have to think. I know. You're not that dark, either. I could just lift you up a few shades. Sound okay?"

"Y-yes."

Topaz went to work. "This sure beats the pink-lady brigade I usually deal with. The Shirley Temple generation."

"Where do you work again?"

"A store called Back Street. You know it, the behemoth of Pasadena. We're even making a Rose Parade float, for Christ's sake. They asked for suggestions and I put *Make it out of thorns*. It's a funny store, though. Like, you know how we handle the money? We get it off the customer, right? And then we put it in these pneumatic-tube things and send it to cash control and plunk! They return the change. That's how far they trust us."

"What about tips?"

"That's different. And I do pretty well. I'm good with the people. I love old people, in fact. They were in the LA that we can only dream of. Not too far from here, there's a vintage-clothing shop next to a nursing home. I mean, what kind of shit is that?"

Topaz towel-dried Pandra's hair with a cloth printed *Property of the Hotel del Coronado*.

Both girls marveled at the new apparition in the mirror. Topaz got her tray of Biba makeup and painted Pandra as if she were playing in a coloring book.

"You know what?" Topaz asked. "There's this contest on KCAT for a model for the *Pin-Ups* billboard to go on Sunset. You get to lean your head on Bowie's pointy shoulder. Well, you know, those shoulder pads he has, with the arrows that go out. Anyway... no one can find those anywhere, by the way—those jackets, I mean. I think Chuckie's going to have one made at Vibrations. But back to the story... you should try!"

"Try?"

"Enter the contest, dodo! You'd be a cinch, especially with me helping you."

"Is this anything like *Hey, kids, let's put on a show!?*" Pandra giggled.

"Now you're catching on! Well, whatcha think?"

Pandra and Topaz arranged to meet at the Century City shopping center at midday on Saturday. The night before, Pandra was anxious to tell her high-school friend, Debbie, of her new adventures. She started a letter, detailing Topaz, Lana Lamé, being an Amber Girl, and lastly and shyly, the billboard contest. Then she elected to hold off mailing the letter until she could add news of the outcome.

The phone rang and it was Topaz.

"I've been thinking about the *Pin-Ups* deal," she said. "When we go to the tryouts, you should let me do the talking. I can be your kind of agent or manager. I think you'll need it, or it could be a good gimmick, anyway. Besides, Lana just told me Mona Best's entering. She'll stop at next to nothing, probably sleep with the judge, that sort of thing."

"But the judge is Lori Lightsout. The deejay."

"That doesn't make a bit of difference! Honey, haven't you heard? This is glitter rock!" Topaz paused. "Anyway, I'd best ring off. Phone bill, you know. If I keep talking to you at this rate, I probably should get one of those tie-line things. Okay, catch ya later."

Pandra hung up, feeling both flattered and confused. One phone call hardly necessitated a reduced-rate phone line. But the notion, plus her new friendship with Topaz and, to a lesser extent, Lana Lamé, thrilled Pandra, who pictured a pair of platform shoes now, with wings on them. Then she heard her sister come in from work.

"I love your hair!" Ellen told Pandra and they embraced like castaways sighting a mirage. "I'd love to do some things like that," Ellen continued, in reference to both Pandra's hair and her contestant status. They shared hot chocolates before drifting off to separate, sugared sleeps.

On Saturday at noon, Pandra squinted in front of a Century City cafeteria. Topaz arrived minutes later, flurrying like the sort of sexpot who'd enter swinging hatboxes and carrying a toy poodle. They went into the cafeteria. "All my customers tell me cafeterias sell the best and cheapest food," Topaz endorsed, slicing into a cheese enchilada on a very hot plate. "But the branch they have downtown is even better. That one has, I kid you not, a waterfall. *And* some rocks and murals. It was built in the 1930s and I think they never turned people away even if they couldn't pay. Something like that."

Pandra, impressed, was also quieted by Topaz's seeming intelligence, her wealth of charmed knowledge.

"I'm surprised I don't see any of the blue-hair brigade here today," she continued, surveying the clientele. "But then this is West LA. They tend to go in more for wigs. Afraid to be their real selves. Don't get me wrong. I'm not saying it's bad to look artificial. Please: I'm not a hypocrite. I just mean, people from the older generation, our parents'... parents, I guess, maybe not that old.... Anyway, they look better stuck in their time and not brought up to date.

"I have this one client, Mrs. Lindstrom, who was some kind of a silent-film star. She wears rhinestone berets and cloche hats and her hair is bobbed, white and fine as silk threads. And she's beautiful. Her scalp is the color of a blanched wooden spool. It is. It'd be awful if she hid it with a wig like some awful sort of husk. That kind of change. I hate change."

"That's funny," Pandra said. "I mean, you transformed me."

"No, that's where you're wrong. All I did was bring out the real you. I didn't cover you up. You had done that yourself."

Topaz drained her 7-Up with a slurp and then the girls paraded around the outdoor mall, taking in Judy's, where Pandra bought a diagonal, off-the-shoulder top. In Vibrations, she selected a pair of cat's-eye sunglasses. The girls then caravaned west in separate cars for the Starwood swap meet where, at Topaz's insistence, Pandra picked up a skirt made from antique scarves, its ragged hem a series of downward diamond points.

The next tour stop was at Fred Slatten Shoes. Displayed in the window, beneath a rotating disco ball, was a pair of white five-inch platforms etched with baby-blue wings. Pandra tried the shoes on, did a trial walk, and then bought them, eyeing the photographs of satisfied customers that dotted the walls, much as cheap, scenic rugs were slung over chain-link fences at major LA intersections.

As they walked out the door, Pandra confessed, "I'm broke now. I don't think I can come out with you guys tonight now. I'd best head home." In truth she had a little more money but she didn't feel quite ready to enter the appliquéd world of her new friends.

"Well, all right then," Topaz allowed. "See you Tuesday, six p.m. sharp. Just come to my place after work and I'll drive you over to the station. After I've gotten you ready, that is."

Back in her car, Pandra aimed south for the flat fields of suburbia. She recalled a pair of shoes she'd seen in a thrift store a couple of days earlier. She'd thought they were platforms, but on closer inspection, they appeared to be made to accommodate a foot deformity.

"Lord Byron had a clubfoot," Ellen had commented. "People found it romantic."

Mona Best looked like a star-crossed angel with strings attached. She had a carny-style beauty: half gypsy, half wax automaton. And Pandra nearly met her again when she replaced her.

"Honey, it's Lana Lamé. I've just heard some news! You watch us on *Real Don*, dontcha? 'Course you do. Well, I've just heard Mona's been kicked off the show. I think she insulted one of the Real Don Steelers or something. I mean, they're sluts anyway, I'm sure they deserved it, but what it adds up to is there's an opening, and Topy and I thought of you. We can get you in, no sweat. Plus you ought to get Mona back for making you lose the Bowie *Pin-Ups* contest."

I didn't lose because of Mona, Pandra thought. Still, she

expressed the desire to try out.

So Pandra prepared for her official debut, further altering herself from sensitive suburban schoolgirl to ruthless glitter moll, a peep-show moth in bulb-mirror sequins and tit-popping tat.

The television show's back-lot soundstage wasn't so different in appearance from the high-school auditorium her friend Debbie had once do-si-do'd in. The girls walked around the lot, Pandra feeling there was something eternally singular about walking—even inside—at dusk, a memory that could only be tied to the uneasy safety, the false security of Halloween: being too small to be out at that evening-still hour, yet protected by the flimsy insulation of costume, of artifice.

In the studio, Pandra clung to Topaz like a gown's cumbersome lace train, easing up only when she tottered in her leopard-and-lucite shoes. On air, she shyly avoided the cameras, an introvert who'd yet to learn how to overcompensate. After the show, Pandra and Topaz found Lana and decided to go to Rodney's English Disco, where as members of the *Don Steele* cast they could get preferential treatment, entering through a fire exit that opened onto an alley behind the Sunset Strip. The hot-wheels flames on Topaz's tube top whirled as she rushed into the mostly empty club. Deceptively crowded with mirror images of the loosely gathered denizens, the room was centered around a few tables and a tiny bar.

Two club stalwarts awaited them: Quinn Highdigger, an impish yet steely gnome, and his sidekick Dan Fisher, who had his own Lazarus-on-stilts act. The former greeted the girls with news of his upcoming mid-December birthday party. "It's also the first anniversary of the club in this location!" he enthused, eyeing Pandra's hair, her unspoiled eyes, and finally her *Aladdin Sane* T-shirt, the Ziggy Flash of which divided her breasts.

"Bowie came here, you know," Quinn addressed her top, his voice a high-pitched grovel. "He wore a dress like on my collector's cover of *The Man Who Sold the World*, and he danced along to Elvis Presley, right over there."

"Bullshit!" Dan scoffed. "You weren't even around that night. You were up, up, and away with Barley Miracle, that chick who says she's the daughter of Marilyn Monroe's half-sister. You had her in the office." He turned to Pandra. "By 'office' I mean the john."

"Not that night," Quinn laughed. "But you really ought to give Barley a record contract."

"As soon as she changes her name to Barely—and gives me a damn good reason. Head, for a start."

Pandra, whose reference points for sex were like term-paper footnotes—every *ibid.* pointing vaguely to Tracy—now felt a rush. Almost intoxicated by her surroundings, she decided sex might be most sustainable in a movie theater. Not a drive-in, that was too clichéd, but in the warped, woven row of a dark and empty cinema, counterpoint to the benevolent beam of a Disneyesque animal romp.

"Mona!" Quinn called out suddenly and, across the narrow square, the minx shrugged her reply.

"She's getting too big for her boobs," Dan sneered, "which isn't saying much." The girls headed for the bar.

"The usual, but this time *three* Shirley Temples," Lana commands.

"Triplets coming up," the barmaid retorted, a touch too wearily for the early hour.

Pandra sipped her drink from twinned red straws and

glanced around. The English Disco had been fashioned by a man who, far from being transatlantic, had rarely even crossed a state line (unless, gossips opined, it involved a minor). A former film-noir watering hole, the tiny club had been hastily remodeled to include a deejay booth, a beer-cooler unit that leaked into the toilets (and vice versa), and a VIP enclave overseen by a picture of Mick Jagger. Black-cherry lip-prints lovedoll-mouthed his rhinestone crotch.

Being in their late teens, Lana, Pandra, and Topaz were elders in the club. Rodney's girls were young but never looked it—the makeup, the life, and the general light in which they moved was harsh and hard and rendered the girls tough as hobnailed boots, effortlessly capable of handling whichever pop star or kinky actor got in their way. One girl sauntered by wearing just two stickers on her flat breasts, bikini panties, and a floppy hat falling over most of her 12-year-old face.

"Shall we take some 'ludes?" Lana asked, but Pandra softly declined. As yet, she was as distant from drugs as she was from lust, but she was close to—right up against—music and as "Panic in Detroit" screeched from the speakers, she rushed by herself to the dance floor where she joined the rest of the club, who'd exited booths and knocked chairs on their sides to come and sway to the song.

During her Monday break from work, Pandra sat under the squat haunches of the All-American Burger. She thought of dancing alone at Rodney's and imagined developing her own sex; neither male nor female nor in between, but exclusionary, her own private language. Rodney had assured her she could enter his club "on the list," and that a well-placed name was like a fine engraving—or a dog tag: all initial noise, giving rise to a lasting impression.

Back in her cubicle, she settled in, preparing to speak clearly into the mouthpiece. She flipped through a short stack of index cards—new clients she'd been assigned. Their details flicked by like a pictograph and then stopped on one, as the remainder fell together. It happened, try after try, in one place, the same place, until Pandra removed the stubborn, stumbling-block card: *Perry Walker*, it read, *Wayward Drive, Hollywood Hills*. As she looked for more, a phone line lit up and she answered to a girl with a tough Valley voice.

"Get Perry on the phone."

"This is his answering service. Would you care to leave a message?"

"Liar. Perry doesn't have an answering service. Who the hell is this?"

"This is Amber Girl Answering. May I take a message for Mr. Walker?"

"Shit. Yeah, this is Mona Best. Tell him to call me at the studio ASAP. And make sure you tell him I won't be here that long. My session's almost over." Pandra took down the number for Cherokee Studios on Fairfax, where Mona, the city's premier bad girl, was presumably rehearsing with a band.

About an hour later, a man called in with an English accent far more understated than Topaz's affected clip. "Peregrine Walker. Any messages for me?"

"Yes, Mr. Walker. Mona Best called at 1:40 from Cherokee Studios, 469-4020. She said she wouldn't be there very long."

"Thanks." He hung up.

At Topaz's that night Pandra told her friend about the call. "Wow! Maybe she's about to launch a group or something. It's playing with fire involving Mona in anything… but maybe you should call in an item to a magazine."

"I can't," Pandra explained. "I'm not supposed to say anything about my calls."

"Blimey, Pandra, don't be so naive! As if Amber Girl cares a damn about you! If you have a story, though I don't think you do yet, sell it! Jesus, I'd sell my grandmother if I could, for some free time. But I don't think there's much market for doddering, doting *abuelas* from Sinaloa."

"I don't know. I could lose my job."

"So? There's plenty of jobs. If I were you, I'd keep my eyes and ears open. You could be eavesdropping on a gold mine one day."

After a few weekly appearances on *Real Don Steele* and then at Rodney's, Lana, Pandra, and Topaz were beginning to gain a reputation. They were perceived as a sexy trio, full of exclusive style and outrageous sass. Through her job at Preview House, Lana got free tickets to a Lakers basketball game, and the girls went decked in their glitter frenzy. Their satin shorts and platform Eldita tennis shoes funhouse-mirrored the players' uniforms.

In the arena's bathroom, which smelled of wet popcorn, a blond girl with curled, center-parted hair spotted the three of them at the sinks and approached.

"I think you guys are really great on *Real Don Steele*. Can I have your autographs?"

The three were thrilled to sign, Lana adding her lip-print to the nubbly brown hand towel that served as an autograph book.

"How do you think up your dances?" the girl asked.

Topaz shrugged and said, "They just come to me," while

Lana scowled slightly.

"We're getting famous, chickadees," the latter chirped on the drive back to Topaz's.

"I knew we would," Topaz replied.

"I think we ought to put in a little more effort, give our fans something to look up to," Lana suggested.

"They have to look up to us with the shoes we wear! I don't know. What do you think, Pan?"

But Pandra, in the back, was asleep, her sparkled forehead vibrating on the armrest of the car door.

In Pandra's dreams swayed an undercurrent of uneasy motion, the discomfort of imperfect escape. She relived, take after take, how she would walk into Rodney's to be greeted each time by what he considered to be her song, the first one she'd danced to there. The memory should have brought the passive, reassuring embrace found in sleep with a secure lover; instead, her rest was that of a confirmed somnambulist—not quite here or there either.

It was as if she slept with a spirit, ineffectual when it came to providing physical comfort. Elusive? No. Impossible? *Always*, said with a barrio gang-slang inflection: *querida*, always! I won't be there for you—always.

A white mantilla was stretched over the chair mated to Topaz's vanity. The head scarf was a throwback to her first communion. She'd unpacked it on learning that her grandmother had arrived and the family would be expected to go to church. Topaz wouldn't wear the mantilla, of course; she only retrieved it to try to remember what she once felt.

In the musty adobe cathedral she recognized Margarito, the altar boy of her childhood, absently kneeling in the pew in front of hers. Over coffee after mass, Topaz broke away from the family table where she had worried lace holes in the hem of the paper table cloth. She approached Margarito, who stood slightly outside a circle of young men more or less his own age.

The night before, she, Pandra, and Lana had done the TV taping, then gone to Rodney's as usual. Afterwards, at Canter's Delicatessen, Lana had announced she was going to Philadelphia, where she was determined to appear on *Soul Train*.

"But *Soul Train* doesn't have any white dancers!" Topaz protested.

"They have one, a Chinese girl, short, with really long hair," Pandra offered.

"She's Japanese, and not very cute," Lana corrected. "You know, the Yoko Ono syndrome."

"How are you going to get there?" asked Topaz.

"I'm going to go-go-go Greyhound. That's how Mona went to New York."

"Is Johnny Thunders really her boyfriend now?" Pandra questioned.

"Well, she traveled back with him on the Dolls' tour bus. Draw your own conclusions."

"Did you know Rodney's got an uncensored copy of the *Diamond Dogs* cover?" Pandra asked, to say something.

"Mona says Bowie's dick is bigger than that," Lana snapped.

"Jesus!" shouted Topaz, slamming the table with her fist. "It's a picture, okay? A drawing of a dog! No one said it was supposed to be real. God, it's not even a photograph! You guys, it's about as realistic as a Ken doll."

"I always used to dress my Ken as a girl," said Pandra. "I

guess I was ahead of my time."

"Hey, kiddo, that's the first boastful thing I've ever heard you say," Lana laughed, putting her arm across Pandra's shoulders as Pandra looked down.

One of the clients Pandra took messages for was a group called the Christian Comfort League, whose mission was "to send the devil into permanent deep sleep." One day, she transcribed a rant alerting the group that "the devil is in disguise" in the form of a commemorative Art Deco sculpture in the center of DeLongpre Park. In haste, Pandra scribbled "disuse" in place of "disguise," causing the CCL's charismatic leader, Zeb Furley, to disregard the plea.

When her error came home to roost, Pandra received her first demerit as an Amber Girl. If she collected three, then she would be demoted, or even removed for a time, like a baseball player. But she failed to take the reprimand to heart, distracted as she was by events closer to her: namely, the falling apart of her friendships. Lana was now ensconced in Philadelphia where she was a focal, if occasional, fixture on *Soul Train*. She could dance, too: real steps, not just swaying side to side in impossible shoes.

Lana was on national TV now, no longer regionalized in the 6 p.m. Southern California weekend slot. This realization dogged Pandra and Topaz, who still shopped for outfits but with lessened zeal. When David Bowie's *Diamond Dogs* tour wound its way to LA, the star was dapper in a double-breasted suit, while his fans squirmed in hot pants and lurex, left awkwardly holding the trick-or-treat bag.

Weeks after the concert, the Hollywood Palladium hosted a Death of Glitter dance at which the New York Dolls played.

Others performed, too: Iggy Pop, plus the GTOs in '60s groupie finery, torn Victorian tart-tat. As a finale, Chuckie was hauled out in a coffin, one sequined shoe dangling over the side. It was a lazy kiss-off to the glitter era, as in too much effort.

"Into the scrapbooks," wrote a rock critic in the *Los Angeles Times*, "and back to the streets." And so it was that the stardust came to settle in the city's gutters, gradually making its way down litter-clogged storm drains, to collect in sewers and form a petri dish for punk.

Pandra and Topaz began to miss tapings of *The Real Don Steele Show*, which was eventually canceled just as Rodney's closed its doors to no one waiting in line.

The last time the girls were all together was at the home of Topaz's sister, on the occasion of Topaz's bridal shower. There were party games; Pandra sat on the tufted carpet and scooped up cotton balls with a spatula.

Mona arrived late, an uninvited guest of honor. She recognized and quickly corralled Pandra and started to tell her about the unwritten agony of being a rock singer's star girlfriend. Paramount in her description was her mettle, her manic will to survive against ugly odds, not the least of which was her heroin addiction.

"How about you?" she challenged. "Are you with anyone?"

"No, no, not me," Pandra responded as Topaz came up, more than a little drunk on sparkling wine.

"Pandra, I was just talking about your mystery phone calls," Topaz said, ignoring Mona. "Have you had any more?"

"*Mystery* calls?" asked Mona.

Pandra didn't get the chance to say she hadn't, before Topaz burbled on about her gifts, her future plans. Finished, she drifted off and Mona eyed Pandra.

"That job you do," she said. "What sort of things do you hear?"

Thus Mona and Pandra formed a queasy alliance, the kind made by the ones left standing. They were the only glitter girls left.

One day at work, Pandra received another panicked call from Mona.

"I have to get word to Perry," she slurred. "I don't have time to wait. You work for him; you've got to help. You've got to come get me at the Woodlawn Motel, Sunset and Highland. You've got to come and help." And Pandra heard a fingernail click—she'd been cut off.

She quickly readied the message for Perry and passed it to Alicia, who agreed to cover for her. Driving the distance to the Woodlawn Motel, Pandra's heart raced. She arrived to find Mona curled on the wet floor of a phone booth, in a pool of aqua-blue shattered glass.

Pandra alerted the motel manager, who looked as if he'd slept in his clothes, hunched over the check-in counter. He arose laboriously, opened the heavy glass door, and crossed the parking lot with Pandra to find Mona sitting up now, holding her head.

"Can you move?" he asked. "Can you walk?"

"I think so," Mona mumbled, as Pandra and the man helped her to her feet. As in a schoolyard game of Blind Man's Bluff, they directed Mona to a room; placed her on a bed where she lay on her side, caressing corn rows of dull green chenille.

"Why don't you sit down?" she hissed at Pandra. Suddenly too hot, Mona removed her leather jeans and the bedspread printed her babyfat thighs.

The door opened to reveal a wan young man of medium height, wearing a satin-trimmed velvet jacket. He approached Mona, nodding to Pandra.

"What took you so long?" Mona asked, choking back tears.

"There, now," he said. "Let's get you out of here." He turned to Pandra. "I'm Perry. I owe you." He searched for his wallet.

"No, that's okay," Pandra replied.

"Tickets then? Guest list?"

"No, really."

Perry, cuddling a protesting Mona in his arms, smiled. "How about dinner, then?"

"Shit, Perry, can't you make your moves on your own time?" Mona said, making an effort to shout.

"Shhh, sweetie." To Pandra: "At least I don't have to ask you for your number!"

And Pandra half smiled, a twinned mask of forced sorrow and comedic thrill.

When Perry called to invite her to dinner, some buried instinct told Pandra what to do. She was sweet, coy, and agreeable: in short, nothing like the person she had been and would be.

In the rustic Cafe Figaro set at the curved end of Melrose Avenue, Pandra picked at her whole-wheat bread and stirred her French onion soup like a sticky cauldron.

"I can't thank you enough for your help with Mona," Perry said, his eyes shiny as his nail polish. His thirties-style patterned shirt had an exaggerated, erotically rounded collar.

"Is she okay now?"

"Yes, right as rain. I should tell you about her, my plans for her. Which, of course, include you."

After Pandra's first kiss with Perry, the desire to take flight loomed as large as a grounded plane she might have boarded. Her urge was to go so far away that only the past would do: she decided to visit Debbie in Oklahoma. She booked a flight, secured the time off work. For the flight she wore a jersey dress patterned with red carnations, linoleum-glitter wedged shoes, and nude stockings with road-movie seams. She was airsick on the flight, too uncertain to trust the support, and when she landed her hair was pressed flaxen.

She spotted Debbie in the picture window, the perfect model of a sexy country cousin: Tammy in bare legs and Bare Traps. Antique silks mixed with gingham and her white elastic-trimmed underpants peeked slyly over the waistband of her jeans, a whitewashed fence touching a mass of blue. Pandra approached the airport lounge nursing a paper cut on her index finger. She had a tendency toward self-mutilation when newly in love: sudden bruised knees, oven burns, cat scratches.

"Pandra!" Debbie shouted, waving wildly. Mack stood just behind her, smoking. Debbie and Pandra embraced, Debbie's numerous bracelets clanking against her thin arms. Mack shook Pandra's hand lightly. Then they bundled Pandra into their economy car and gave the tired traveler an exhaustive tour of their city, particularly its cruising main drag, McAllister Street.

"We'll bring you here Saturday night," Debbie assured.

"You'll laugh your head off. Can you believe this is what passes for something to do around here? And we thought we had it bad in Orange County!"

When they arrived at the woodland-motif apartment (even its wallpaper depicted a forest), Mack gave Pandra a cup of sugary herbal tea and rolled her a joint. Debbie rushed in and out of the bedroom carrying armfuls of her clothes, their hangers glinting in the overhead light. Pandra ooh'd and ah'd in the appropriate places, fingering the fabrics as if they were scarce tickets.

She slept that night on a four-foot loveseat and dreamt she was on a plastic raft adrift in a lake, seeing Perry's face in an imperfect light. Its flaws were exposed, as happens with extreme beauty. Turned a hair, he's breathtaking; another, asymmetrically askew. And she turned herself, until the lake became a sea, an ocean.

A vision of Pandra draped on a settee, looking like a figure on the side of an Art Nouveau vase. Even her body curls in the right places.

She's with a therapist, Dr. Anton. And as she drifts she hears him remind her she is a murderess. As she lands he tells her she is fine, and will forget.

Dr. Anton is a professional friend of Perry, Pandra's then husband who'd appeared and rescued her—married her at a time when she was lost, had gone from answering-service clerk to groupie-cum-call-girl under the guidance of Hollywood kid Lance Allowed. With Mona as the main conduit, she had slipped and slept (well, sometimes she shut her eyes) through a score of clients, often in tandem with Mona but progressively alone, on show. The agency, Come-a-Lot, was a brainchild of

Perry's and gave Mona a way of supplementing her heroin habit more adequately than her new band, the Black Dahlias, who nonetheless were getting some FM airplay with their LP, *Emancipated Minor*.

As Pandra later learned, Perry suggested the plan to Mona at Barney's Beanery on Santa Monica Boulevard as she sat across from him, trying to read the irrelevant newspaper clippings pressed beneath the laminated tabletop. She was dressed in worn black leather and slurped a strawberry shake through a clown-striped straw.

"Fuck!" she hissed. "It's easier giving blow jobs than getting a sip of this drink."

"Shhh, Mona," Perry said. "Don't you ever get sick of the groupie trip? I mean, don't you think you should be getting more out of it?"

"I'm not a goddamn groupie, okay?"

"No, I know. You're a rising star. We all know that. But it's just that I know you're always looking for money—and don't you think that every moment of your life, somehow, you should be getting paid for it, just because of who you are?"

"Yeah, but I thought that's why you put together the Black Dahlias, even though they're a bunch of peroxide bitches except for me, and even though I said I wanted to go solo like Suzi Quatro."

"Well, Mona, it could be quite some time before we see any real money."

"Then why can't we print some? And what about this picture sleeve for the next single, SWAK? What were you thinking, the girls around me, me in the center..."

"A singing raven in a nest of..."

"Straw!" laughed Mona.

"But Mona, these things have to be paid for and we simply do not have the money yet."

"Then I'll have to find another manager."

"Now, you know no one has my vision, no one can see that you get to where I'm going to take you. But if you think you'd like to try and find out what the business is like without me, just go right ahead. I'd see you in oblivion, baby, except I won't be there." Perry picked up the check.

"Wait, no, wait," Mona stammered, her forehead sweating. "What do you mean, get some money? If you're talking about turning tricks, I've already done it. It's shit."

"It wouldn't be like that," Perry said softly. "You know I'd always take care of you, look after you."

"Well, what do you mean then?"

And Perry detailed his vision of Come-a-Lot, ending with a plea. "We need some more girls, Mona. I was thinking of Pandra."

"Who? Oh, her. Well, she's hardly going places. The only thing is, she seems completely sex-dead to me. But then, feeling sexy isn't a requirement for the job, is it? I mean, this whole scene's about faking it. Do you want to ask her or should I?"

Back at Amber Girl after her trip to Oklahoma, Pandra was removing her headset before going on a break when the boss's secretary appeared under the fluorescent lights, casting a shadow over Pandra's in-tray.

"Mr. Tarmack wants to see you," the woman said. The rhinestone initials at the corners of her glasses winked in the fractured light. "Why don't you come with me?"

In the corner office, Pandra waited to be invited to sit down.

"Pandra," Mr. Tarmack said, slightly raising his balding head to peer into her eyes, "it appears you have misplaced a number of messages of late—or failed to deliver them at all." He looked directly at her now, without blinking.

Pandra was surprised, didn't think she had.

"The standard reprimand for that is three weeks' suspension without pay."

She gasped internally, having just moved into a studio apartment above a guitar shop in a downtrodden part of the Strip. She would have been all right had she still lived at home, but having left home and Ellen, she knew there was no going back. Those who returned to Orange County never got out again. Still, she would have to find a way to pay the rent.

"You're entitled to work for the rest of this pay period," he continued, "but then you're on your own until your re-entry date which would be..." he thumbed through the loose leaves of a desk calendar while counting to himself in audible whispers, "September 17. And on that day, we'd expect a change in attitude."

Pandra had no reply, and was told that was all. She cleared her desk, certain she wouldn't be back.

That night, dressing to go out, she put on satin hot pants, the double seams of which rubbed like her body turned suddenly in on itself. She went to the Rainbow, for want of anywhere else to go. In the lot outside, at the bottom of the stairway leading to On the Rox, she spied Mona talking to a basketball player, who was crouching down to hear her.

Inside the bar, Pandra was waved over by Perry, whose face was partially obscured by a tilted bottle of champagne swimming in a silver bucket. "Sit down," he beckoned. "This is Lance." A young man with a pageboy cut nodded. "And this is Rory Otis." The latter winced as he momentarily removed his sunglasses to reveal ringed eyes.

"I saw Mona outside," Pandra said.

"Oh, yeah, she'll be here later." Perry went on, "Rory here is the next Dylan. He lives and writes in the desert, in an adobe house."

"Motel," Rory corrected, adjusting his unraveling cork-screw perm.

Pandra smiled; there was nothing to say about her own life. She downed several Bacardi and cokes in succession, the tumblers never resting on the tabletop as business was discussed. Pandra was dizzy, otherworldly. In response to the men, she tilted her head to one side as if asking for affection.

Lance, she pieced together, was placing ads in the *Free Press* about a call-girl agency he was starting. Pandra went along with it, for some reason thinking about a childhood memory: bleached patches on the front lawn made by newspapers left for days, then thrown away unread.

"That chick gave the biggest hickeys," Lance was laughing, "and I'm not saying where." But Pandra continued to see splotchy green, dichondra choked by crabgrass. By the time she got up to leave with Perry, she'd forgotten to ask why Mona had never arrived.

Perry's apartment was high above the Strip, its brick balcony boasting a backdrop of sky and several neglected potted plants. His bed was in the front room; the bedroom he used as an office. Pandra took off her short velvet jacket, New York T-shirt, glossy underwired bra. Her satin shorts she kept on. When Perry unhooked her fishnets, the garters flapped like bath-time rubber-duck bills.

His lips touched her nipples, his hands went to and fro on

her satin crotch. The seams soon overtook her nylon, cotton-lined bikini underwear and felt like a ridge before the fabric-covered protrusion was inside her. Perry tried to work his way around the clothes, but became embroiled in the underwear, pushing at it like a cheesecloth veil, a cover keeping the food safe at a muggy summer picnic.

"It's a funny way to lose your virginity," Perry said. "Technically, you may still be pure." But Pandra wasn't listening; she was choosing her feelings: the culmination of her past, questions about her future.

In the weeks that followed, Pandra was in the depths of sex. It was how she fell into Lance's prostitution circuit, out of longing for a physicality that Perry now denied her.

Lance ran his agency out of a guest house in Laurel Canyon. The ceilings had hooks intended for macramé plants—now, reinforced, they supported various S&M arrangements. Lance also sold clothes: when his girls weren't working, they were stitching sequins to jackets, like characters trapped in the unhappy part of a fairy tale. Many of the girls were also on drugs, but for Pandra it was sex, solely the feeling of penetration, that singular moment. She detested foreplay, the rest.

"That's because you started masturbating really young," another girl, Janine, told her.

Pandra failed to recognize the dangers of her life, thinking Lance and Perry would look after her. Now she could pay for her studio apartment and sleep the day away, even through the guitar lessons on the floor below. And the men she slept with weren't so bad—they were older than she; still, she ignored all but the most appalling appearance in favor of her private moment, which she always kept to herself.

And while the other girls had stories of close calls, violence, impossible demands, Pandra had none.

"That's because you're Perry's favorite," Janine said. "He's saving you."

One night Mona and Pandra were alone, as if aloft in a treehouse. Mona, high as usual, was without a career now. "No career, no cares," she sputtered as the phone rang and she rushed to it too fast. Pandra supposed Mona thought it was her latest rock boyfriend.

"Shit, Perry," she said. "It's only you. What? Okay, I'll ask her. But how do we get out there...? What? Yeah, sure."

On the two-lane road to Twentynine Palms, Pandra felt she should be noticing the Joshua trees and crippled cacti, thinking about how during a *chubasco* they would rustle like wired snakes on a dark ride. But these thoughts mostly eluded her; she looked now and then at Mona, and tried to picture Perry driving. He looked best in profile.

"It's as if he really *is* two halves," she said to Mona, who was steering with both hands together at the bottom of the wheel. "And it's his hidden side that gets to me."

"Oh, Pandra, please shut up. Seriously, I can't take this romance bullshit. You only think these things because you're in it. The view from over here is not as pretty, I can assure you. Perry's a creep, Pandra, he's using you. That's the whole point of him, of his job, even. That's how he gets by: living off others. I mean, just look at yourself, will you? You're in a shitty car driving to a sleazy motel in the middle of the end of nowhere and you're going to fuck someone you've barely met. For money, most of which you won't see. And yet you're trying to make something beautiful out of it."

"Maybe I think beauty is truth."

"Oh, help me. Life isn't high-school English class. It isn't the cheerleading squad, either. I wonder if you'll ever wise up."

"Let's just drop it, okay?" Pandra said. "I wouldn't expect you to understand."

The Twilight Motel had several Joshua trees in its bungalow courtyard. Their arms pointed in conflicting directions.

After parking the car in the diagonal slot, the girls looked the other way from the registration office—No Vacancy, its reception window boded—and headed for Room 7 of the L-shaped, one-story motel. Mona rapped on the door with the summit of her oversized rhinestone ring. It was opened by a guy who looked like a linebacker, only bigger. She brushed him aside and ducked under his gigantic biceps. Rory was in the tiled kitchenette, an open carton of eggs on the formica table. He walked toward them, twisting his lanky perm into a rubber-banded knot.

"Let's get down," Mona commanded.

"Casey, take a hike," Rory said. "Go into Twenty-nine Palms and fight with some Marines—or better still, find out what else they do for fun."

He turned to the girls. "Hey, I'm Rory. What are your names again?" He extended one hand, the knuckles of which were covered by narrow slabs of turquoise set in single silver bands. A squash-blossom necklace jiggled on his chest.

"Mona Best. And this is Pandra."

"M&P, or P&M, just the thing to get me through the night," Rory said. "Can I get you anything, M&P? I'm having an omelet myself."

"Nah," said Mona. "Let me fix it for you." She levered

the spatula from his skinny hand, then rested it on the stove top as she flung off her jacket, struggling her tube top over her head. She smiled as she cooked topless. "I know what you're thinking," she sassed. "My tits are so flat they're like two fried eggs. No one's ever called me Mona Breasts. Well, not in a nice way, at least."

"I wasn't going to say..." started Rory.

"I've heard it all before, too many times. Just sit down, sir, and you'll be served in no time."

Pandra sat down in a naugahyde chair placed next to a twinned nightstand. Mona spoon-fed Rory, straddling his lap as she balanced to maintain her position on the high-perch bar stool.

Next, tumblers of vodka, lines of cocaine, displayed like the contents of a broken snow dome.

"Pandra here was homecoming queen," Mona told Rory, who nodded his head to hit the vinyl-padded headboard.

"She must have some real good moves."

As Pandra turned to Rory she thought of nothing at all. In Mona's arms she wanted to struggle free but instead buried her face in her neck, her armpit, any crevice from which she wouldn't have to look up.

Mona tantalized Rory with her ostrich boas, ticked him off with her tongue. He tied his upper arm as he shot up while the girls sat cross-legged on the bed, watching Johnny Carson. Mona declined the needle with a shake of her head, but when Rory pressed its point to Pandra's wrist, she jerked away and then reeled forward, toppling Rory off the bed. His head hit the peeling corner of the nightstand. A tiny tear of blood beaded like the lit message bulb atop the bedside telephone, which also fell alongside Rory, its corkscrew cord entwining with his hair and landing like a whimsical version of the rubber tube now lying limp on the floor.

"You could hear music in that." Mona meant the rumble, the phone's off-kilter clang, and the thud Rory had made. "But I think it spells trouble," she said a moment later. "Could be this turkey's done."

Pandra scrambled off the bed and grabbed Rory's wrist. "I can't feel a pulse," she cried in panic after a few seconds.

"We've got to get out of here," said Mona.

"Hey, can you hear me?" Pandra called, leaning over Rory.

"Oh please. Let's just get out of here."

"Shouldn't we get help?"

"Why? He's already helped himself."

And they headed for the car, Mona checking the bathroom to see if she'd left anything.

In front of Pandra's apartment, Mona said, "Don't call me and I won't call you."

"Who's going to tell Perry?"

"Perry's the least of our problems. Let him come to you. Just stay in. Look, I don't know. I think I'm going to hit the road, see who's going on tour. I think Silverhead are and I'm sure I could hitch my tail to their wagon, or something like that. But you and me should avoid each other. You know how to do that, Pandra. Remember those kids smoking in the bathrooms at recess? The ones you never wanted to acknowledge existed? Just think of them all as me."

"I wasn't like that," Pandra defended. "I was always nice to everyone."

"I give up. See you in the funny papers—or at least in *Rock Scene*."

In her apartment, Pandra set down her bag and fell into bed with her shoes on. The next thing she remembered, there was a knock at the door. She opened it chain-length and saw Perry.

"Rory's gone. Get packed. I'm taking you to Mexico."

"My bag's over there."

"Good girl. Let's ride." As they drove east and then south, Pandra sobbed without making a sound.

In the tiny village of Santa Sofia, curled up against the Sea of Cortez, Pandra and Perry played out an overacted summer. They fell exaggeratedly in love, kissing while sunbathing, cuddling while skinny-dipping, Pandra atop his shoulders as if she were at a rock festival.

"Rory's actually more valuable to me if he's not around," Perry said to Pandra as they drove to La Paz. "It was getting harder and harder to keep him out of the press—and out of jail—with the drugs and everything. And he wasn't writing. He'd never have delivered that next record. If we play the mysterious disappearance angle right, he might end up a bigger star than he could ever have been if he were still with us."

Pandra nodded her head dashboard dachshund–style and then lowered it, a novelty ostrich bobbing over a water glass, to give Perry a blow job.

By the time they returned to Los Angeles that fall, Pandra and Perry were engaged, Mona was nowhere to be found, and Rory's records were climbing the charts like a beanstalk up a trellis. Pandra began to find her picture in tabloids like the *National Intruder,* photos taken as she accompanied the now famous Perry to clubs and parties. She looked at her grainy face, her image permanently out of focus and in a duplicitous register, as if she had a ghost.

The papers also documented their upcoming nuptials, to be held at the Chelsea Hotel in New York, presided over by Honey Mink—a drag queen, Mainman artiste, former Warhol accessory, and ordained Pentecostal minister. On the morning of the wedding, the New York Post bannered, THE BRIDE WILL BE CHANGING HER MIND over a picture of Perry embracing Mona at Max's Kansas City. Pandra knew it was from the stag night, but couldn't help staring at Mona's photogenic squalor, her strip-club tat and plaything pout.

Pandra lived with Perry in the Los Angeles foothills, her body now pregnant as Mount Hollywood's plump profile. Jobless and isolated, she lived for news of her husband's day and shrugged when he lashed out. Her bruises faded slowly.

Their daughter, Moxy, was born in Children's Hospital on the day Elvis Presley died, smack-dab in the middle of the Summer of Hate. When Pandra gave her child up for adoption, she felt as if she'd been handed one thousand words for sorrow; yet none of them came close. She kept seeing her daughter in her buggy, tucked in on the eiderdown side of life. Or sitting in her crib, using the bars to pull herself up, eventually thinking the TV commercials were speaking to her.

Mona turned up dead in a New Orleans hotel, but her passing was barely a footnote in a rock-and-roll anthology. Pandra imagined Mona's body being brought back somehow by Perry, to occupy a shrine in a dark ride at the rock and roll theme park he was apparently now planning.

Pandra moved in with Reese, whom she'd met in a library as he strolled past the books with elaborate disinterest. He'd declared his love for her in a laundromat, abstractedly removing cufflinks that read *hot* and *cold* the way some knuckles said *love* and *hate*. "With me," he'd said, "everything has a happy ending." Pandra had believed him so much she felt like writing her own story.

WHY?" STROOD ASKS Giselle. "Why did Pandra Jane write this whole thing in the third person?"

"You'd have to meet her. She always refers to herself in the third person. 'Pandra wants to go here, Pandra would like that, that's something Pandra would wear.' It's eerie." Giselle applies a globule of Liquid Paper to a fledgling run in her tights. "In fact, that reminds me, I have to call her today. Another thing I hate doing. When she picks up, you can just hear the anticipated disappointment in her voice."

"What are you going to say about the manuscript?"

"You tell me."

"I think it's good, but like your tights—kind of opaque. And after that Rory guy dies, she can't keep up an interest in her tale."

"Oh, God, that, too. I have to call my cat author. But did you find the story believable? Sometimes I'm really not sure…"

"I don't know about that. I think the book is good, though. Maybe she could be a kind of retro star—not a youthquaker, but an agequaker."

"Strood, the best we can hope for in these times is an end to all Warholisms," Giselle replies. "I'd rather you'd quote P.T. Barnum or W.C. Fields or H.L. Mencken. But you might be right about Pandra."

"I am," attests Violet. "But the book is a little short."

"That's what photographs are for," says Giselle. "Still, I'm hoping she can flesh it out a little more." She picks up the phone and punches Memory 06. What she hears is a message.

Pandra would like you to know she's away, in the last bastion of lost and found love.

That's Pandra all over, thinks Giselle. Even when good news bites, she's unavailable, tenuous to track down, playing a soap-opera heroine to Giselle's dishwater hands. It's a mystery where Pandra is; but Giselle feels if it's about love, she'll give it a wide berth.

As if on auto-cue, Violet buzzes through on the intercom— though the office is so small a whisper would have sufficed. "I've got Len on the line," she nearly sings, "and he sounds mighty full of himself."

Giselle sighs. "I'll take him."

"My little gazelle," says a voice with the texture of loose tobacco. "I've got myself a job, but I'll still be free nights. It's part-time, but it just about makes the one-bedroom rent. Want to know what it is?"

"Sure, Len."

"I'm rounding up shopping carts for Stater Brothers—the parking lot and beyond. Sometimes I take a truck out. The way I see it, it's kind of a saga, me gathering the herd. The last roundup. Only wish I could use my lasso."

"Len, are you sure about this?" asks Giselle as she starts to think ahead. "But wait a minute. Stater's has this marketing campaign, don't they? *The Heartland*, and *Where America Shops*."

"And they bag in paper, not that breakaway plastic b.s."

"Well done, Len! I can really run with this!"

"Honey, I love it when you talk about leaving. Now how about a celebratory drink tonight at the KO Korral?"

Giselle knows she can say no to everyone but Len. Still, she can try to resist. "I don't know. I couldn't make it till later."

"Ten?"

"Ten-thirty."

"See you there, my little misfit."

Giselle's cheeks flush. Len often thinks of her as the Marilyn Monroe character in Monroe's last complete film. He, of course, is Clark Gable, though the resemblance is no greater than the Warren Oates one Giselle superimposes on him. Len is, in fact, a chubby chipmunk: a large man with a cartoon face like a benevolent 1930s comic-book moon.

In performance, he is as patchy as Neil Young's old jeans, but the songs he writes are firmament jewels: "Highway Hypnosis" and "Daddy Loves a Six-Pack But Mama's Got a Six-Gun" have a kind of squalid beauty; imbued with his harplike twang, they conjure cotton clouds cut by slow-swirling ceiling fans.

It is his vision she loves, a thing which can't be touched. That, and his kisses like an outlaw's fingertips—wanted but unprintable.

Giselle replaces the receiver and briefly wonders how she'll endure the minutes until 10:30. But the luxury of longing is short-lived in her crowded, hectic world, and she quickly gets up to make a cup of Sleepytime tea, though it's not yet midday. Back at her desk, she smoothes her A-line skirt, which she'd laughingly told Strood she made a beeline for at a sale.

Looking at her agenda, she readies for a meeting with Brad, a screenwriter. "An appropriate name," Giselle remarks, and Strood says, "I don't get it."

"You know, scripts. They're bound with brads."

He appears in the doorway now, wearing tortoise-shell glasses that make light of his rugged looks, as if he were calculatedly wooing a wider audience. He deposits his script in Giselle's in-tray (which she's labeled "intrigued"), and begins his underhand softball pitch.

"It's about this actress/model/waitress who does a man-in-the-street interview on a TV news show. She's reacting to a Rodeo Drive heist. The perpetrators see her and think she knows too much. In reality, she was just hamming it up, ad-libbing. You know, in case this is her big break, she wants Mr. DeMille to know she's ready for her close-up."

"I'm with you."

"Also watching is a nutcase who instantly becomes obsessed with her. Her boyfriend also catches her appearance and is embarrassed by it—it's the last straw for him. He leaves her just as the others start stalking. But it's funny, too, like *Home Alone* meets... I don't know, I still need to fill in that blank."

"It'll come to me. You said you've done other stuff?"

"Equity-waiver theater, a couple of pilots for cable."

"What happened there?"

"Crash landing." Brad makes a diving sound effect.

"You'll hear from me soon." Giselle bends to place the script in the schoolgirl satchel under her desk. But it's just out of reach: she's kicked it over, along with the wicker wastepaper basket. As she crawls into the wooden cubby, she's put in mind of Sidonia, cat author, who believes her cat exists for the sole purpose of enticing her to make a fool of herself on the floor.

"I tell you, he contrives these situations just to humiliate me, to bring me down to his level where I can't possibly compete," she'd said. "Once I comply, he smirks and turns away, tail in the air, laughing to himself at the way I move."

"Sounds like an analogy for love to me," Giselle had retorted, then suggested Sidonia tackle a self-help book on romance. "Maybe you could work up something like 'people-combining,' using the principles of food pairing—you know, red beans and rice to form a perfect protein—then applying it to what one needs for the ideal relationship."

She'd paused then, thinking better of it.

"But maybe love's got nothing to do with protein. Anyway, don't listen to me. I'm hardly the romantically balanced woman."

In the KO Korral, Giselle toys with a flat bar coke; buoyed in its center is an evil-looking maraschino cherry. She waits for Len to return from the lone pay phone, hoping he doesn't slip on the alternately slick and sticky wooden floor. So fraught with pratfalls is their time together that she's certain it's symbolic, a metaphor. Perhaps that's another thing she likes about him; why she loves him so much.

Len lumbers into view, jolly as Babe, Paul Bunyan's blue ox. As he turns to acknowledge a friend, the expanse of his elbow picks off a stein of Hamm's from a rickety railing and sends it cascading to the floor as vividly as a waterfall on any old beer sign.

"Hey, I'm sorry," Len says to the aggrieved drinker. "I'm afraid I'm just a bull in a... well, you can't exactly call the KO Korral a china shop."

"More like a bull in a shithole," the young man responds, slow to accept the apology.

"Let me replace that for you—and raise you one."

"Deal."

Giselle watches the exchange from her leatherette barstool, crossing her legs to try and appear less uncomfortably perched.

"Well, then, how's my sweetie pea?" Len grins at Giselle and she's suddenly weightless, a trapeze girl confident she'll be caught.

"Okay, Len."

"Sure?"

"Okay, you're right. I'm a little down—just another nasty review for Adon. *Tearaway* said he was 'in possession of a talent curiously less than his years.'"

"That's not so bad. The kid's a teen idol, not Orson Welles."

"I still think it's hard on him, all this criticism. But then I guess he can cry buckets of tears into the twin seats of his new T-bird."

"He got a 'bird? I didn't even know he had a learner's permit." Len draws on his longneck.

"Adon's doing really well for me... for us, since what's good for the golden goose..."

"Is good for the gilded gander. Listen here, my next gig is going to be something extra special, you'll see. What say we get out of here, and I'll tell you about it. Your back forty or mine?"

"It would help for me to be home in the morning. I've got an early meeting with Hedda Hophead, who's appointed herself majordomo of a band called the Glee Club."

"Meaning?" Len puts his bottle on the edge of the bar and Giselle nudges it closer to the middle.

"You know, those all-male vocal groups in ivy-strewn 1920s colleges. Glee Clubs."

"Not that, the major dodo."

"Oh, Len, stop playing dumb." She kisses the soft sachet of his cheek.

"But if Hedda's the ringleader, what's your part?"

"Lion tamer? Fire swallower?"

Len gulps, puts the empty bottle to his lip and exaggeratedly strains at the dewy air. "I'll drink to that—at the temple of your wet bar."

Giselle's apartment is small but affords her a view: molting palm trees, motionless cement lakes, blanket-stitched railroad tracks to the left; to the right, shiny billboards, streaky car lights, defiant skyscrapers, and the ambivalent slaps of the Pacific Ocean rebuking the city's relentless, cold advances. She opens her front door, aware as always that she doesn't have a pet but wants one. Instead she has Crazing, her agency: a picture hanging in the hall shows her charges ranged like a class photo, with her, back row center, the slightly embarrassed teacher.

"Coffee? Tea? Me?" she asks as she mimes holding a tray while trying to walk a straight line.

But Len smoothes the affectation from her face and off her broad, tensed shoulders.

At dawn she wakes up in bed, boxed in by his body, the wall, her vinyl and chintz headboard. At her feet the quilt is coiled. Unfurled, it might reveal Cleopatra—or at least her high-cut underwear, a single bleached sports sock nestled between Len's slinky tuxedo pair. Len turns and then curls, providing Giselle a window of easy escape. "No," he mumbles, asleep. "I asked for 'The Twelfth of Never.'"

Shivering in the coverless chill of morning, Giselle goes to make the vanilla-bean coffee. If he doesn't love her, she broods as the drag of her slippers catches on the harelip of the aged linoleum floor, if he so much as doesn't, he'll get his. She's older than he is, it's true, but she'll age better. So if he's considering packing her off for a younger version, once he's hit the big time, she'll still be all right.

No, you won't, something tells her, but she knows it's an admonishment that's like a camera: it doesn't lie, but the results can be retouched.

Awake in the next room, Len is thinking back to his days as a bouncer. Gig, he'd called himself, Gig Middles. Part live wire, part dead as a doorman. He'd led a life of precision poverty, his closet skeletons as visible as those in an anatomy lecture. He'd stood guard, a cigar-store Indian, night after night at Studio 45: Bismarck, North Dakota's dyslexic, belated answer to New York City's premier disco.

Too old to mount Hollywood, too young to Forest Yawn, he'd gone for a drive one day, taking the long way. Deciding to park, he found his wheels climbing the curb and hoped no one saw. On that cold afternoon, outside a coffee shop, the genie of epiphany had appeared. What had eluded him in life was that it was never high noon. So he took brisk two-steps to rectify that, heading west for the only land still promised.

Giselle enters the room, carrying two mugs of coffee. She opens the heavy drapes to let in a controlled line of light, a slat in the pulley curtains. Staged as an arena show, their bodies move together in and out of this demarcation, a long scratch on a baize pool table. They come to rest apart in the felt dark.

"I've got to get going," Giselle says finally. "Thanks for the kick start."

"My pleasure, my sweetness trough, my trembling tickle-bee," Len says, far off, as if he were playing word association in order to write a lyric.

Giselle drives to the office, wondering whether their separate work would always make each feel the other belonged to some insatiable enticement, or unrequited obsession. As she parks in the rock-bordered gravel space, so like the ones in the Gingham Ghost Town amusement park of her childhood, she feels unprepared. Hedda will come in guns blazing, speaking an impenetrable lingo that Giselle might have had a key to if she'd only sidestepped the KO Korral the night before (staying for one drink, then going home alone).

In front of her single-story building, throwing rocks onto the hasty Zen garden of the roof, is Hedda in a short plaid skirt, plaits, and bother boots. "Oh!" she says, spying Giselle. "Sorry. I was getting anxious. Did I mess it up, the roof?"

"I'm not sure there's anything to mess up. But those rocks you added, the garden variety ones, will be at odds with the calcite white ones that are already up there. So who knows what kind of turmoil you may have caused!"

Hedda shrugs, noses another pebble with the toe of her boot. "Stuff like that always happens to me."

Inside, aggressive as junk mail and just as relentless, Hedda shoves a glossy at Giselle. "Glee Club, new lineup."

Giselle looks, knits her brow. What had been four top-drawer, clean-cut boys were now three disheveled cellar-dwelling girls, with glares like feedback off mirrored sunglasses at scorching midday.

"I fired the guys," Hedda says. "Maybe the best way to

explain it is if you come out to where we live."

Giselle doesn't answer, isn't anxious to travel south to La Milagra, a sleep-still suburb where the only movement is accidental, involuntary.

"I guess I oughta say, too, that I wrote to RSVP to see if they're interested."

Hearing this, Giselle blinks five times in rapid succession. RSVP is Crazing's main rival in the eccentric-but-influential personal manager stakes. "I'll consult my organizer," she says. "Strood? When am I free?"

Having secured a meeting, Hedda leaves the office for Hollywood Boulevard, where she'll catch a bus downtown. Once there, she'll transfer to an express bus whose final destination is the sparsely sparkled parking lot of an amusement park called Fancy Free. Then, once she crosses the road gridlocked with cars detouring a freeway interchange, Hedda will be home.

Hedda is a long young woman who fled the perfect, three-bedroom family to live in a rat-dominated former motel. Reminders of the rodents ellipsis across the thin carpet. The flimsy front door is flagged by two tumbleweeds blown there in a storm and now clinging to resilient dead shrubs that refuse to be uprooted. Hedda sleeps across the wide street from the rundown, derelict Fancy Free park.

Like Hedda, it's neither fancy nor free. Of an uncharted but wizened age she cites as *umpteen*, Hedda carries out the rituals of the wily dispossessed: she schemes. She also does her best to avoid the building manager, hanging judge for a landlord named Johnny Cliff.

Other than that, it's okay. She gets away from her dullifying past here, and cavorts near the wiggly concrete fields and paint-peeling ice-cream mountains of Fancy Free, the perimeters of which are lassoed by a monoxide noose of cars trying to gain access to the freeway on-ramp without being forced through the main park gates.

Hedda doesn't *fear* as so many people do. Her world is like a royal maze, her own peculiar method of interacting with nature, a kind of ordered terror that turns in on her. And she is former leader of a gaggle, a girl gang who worked the cartoon streets and awarded each other merit badges based on all the wrongs they'd achieved. Once the emblems began to hang heavy on their sagging ornamental sashes, the girls splintered off, leaving behind a remnant of four, including Hedda.

And although Hedda is the hardest, she has a weak link: her fondness for the early 1960s, particularly girl groups singing about ill-fated love. In that light, it seems preordained that she would exchange the *16 Magazine*–shiny, Clearex-matted complexions of the male Glee Club for a female version: hard eyes beckoning with flippant eyeliner, filthy mouths puckering with Maybelline's In the Pink lipstick.

The girls—Annette FunCity, Tammy Whynot, and Doris Dismay—look up to Hedda, while admitting to each other she's no one they'd want to exchange Christmas cards with. No, she's the kind of girl who'd give away personally dedicated books, who'd abandon her once-prized pastel autograph book, who'd use her ancestors' somber occasional photographs as sepia heirloom confetti.

Giselle arrives to meet the girls in a teriyaki coffee shop. Smells of wet linoleum, hash-brown grease, and soy sauce form a not unpleasant mixture.

"Okay," Hedda commands. "Let me introduce Annette, Tammy, and Doris: the Glee Club." Giselle nods but her gaze stays a moment on Tammy, whose fringed, blanket-patterned boy's shirt Len would love. But what would he make of her eyes, pastel yet hard-boiled, like a not quite successful Easter egg?

"Tammy used to be a lot lizard."

"She probably doesn't know what one is," Tammy says to Hedda.

"Let me surprise you," Giselle corrects. "It means you worked the truck stops—turned tricks with truckers in their cabs during stopovers."

"Ching-ding-ching-ding," Tammy says, imitating a pinball machine. "One free game."

Giselle refuses to be unnerved. "What's your plan?"

"Well, I'll guide 'em to stardom," Hedda enthuses. "And you can help me, get the press and stuff."

"I'm usually more of a manager," she says in a brave attempt to shirk responsibility. Annette and Doris stare each other down over the last chili fry. "But in this case, I could leave the managing to you."

"We've got a new demo. Annette, where's your Walkman?"

Annette squirms in her muumuu, and ducks under the table for her straw bag, which has blue starfish and pink sand dollars pinned down the side in plastic casing. Her Walkman, though, is thoroughly modern. Annette fixes the intricate earpieces to Giselle's ears. Shortly she hears a heathen barrage, an ethereal wail, the sound of a siren trapped in a conch shell.

"If you drive in (drive in, drive in), don't forget to visit the snack [handclap] bar," goes the lyric; but it's the afterburn echo that stays with Giselle, and prompts her to announce: "Let's do some work."

"We've got covers, too," Hedda adds.

"What about live dates?"

"Oh, no. No, no. Not till we're top of the hit parade. Not till we're *Name That Tune*."

"In two notes," Tammy adds, sipping Tabasco sauce from a spoon as if it were bad medicine.

Making pasta that night, Giselle sighs along with the curlicues as they hit the bubbling water. It is the sound of surrender one reserves for an alter ego. She rapidly ponders: Is that Len? Is it another? And it's this heightened claustrophobia that prompts her to slump on the zebra-patterned barstool, holding a carrot in her hand like a sorry microphone. She cries briefly and quietly, over layers of wrongs and misstatements she's committed in love—not life, for her work, she feels, is inviolate. It's not like the fluff at the top of a pill bottle; it's the relief, and a kind of verbal trampoline to the future combined with a preservation order on the present. The past? Well, that was something one exaggerated, or wrote off altogether.

After a long evening of TV, Giselle falls asleep curled in a rocking chair, her mother's childhood quilt swaddled at her slender feet. A rap at the door startles her. Only the milkman in "Lullaby of Broadway" is up at this hour. She walks to the front door, where she peers through the peephole, prepared to see a peaked cap. But it's black instead of dairy white, garnished with candy-wrapper gold braid.

"Western Union," says a young man through the door. Giselle opens to greet his spotty yet evocative face. He is a handsome imp. "Telegram for Miss Entwistle."

"Thanks," Giselle says, excusing herself as she turns to the entryway table where a Sands Casino ashtray sits, filled with spare change and dollar bills furled like the rubber rims of dinghies. Turning back, she says "I'm curious…"

"Most people are when they get a telegram."

"Oh, no, that can wait. No, I'm just wondering what provoked, what prompted you to take this job?"

"It's a long story, but mostly I like to watch people's reaction shots. This is only one of my jobs."

"Maybe this is against the rules, but would you like to come in for coffee? It's just that I'm interested in stories outside the norm, things like this." Giselle experiences a sudden flush of shyness, as if she were a mythical bored housewife looking for love. "I mean, I'm not going to make a pass at you or anything."

The young man laughs, partially revealing a set of perfect, tiny teeth. "I like mine with warmed-up milk."

Giselle stares.

"My coffee."

"Of course." She flaps the telegram like a southern belle's nonchalant fan. "I suppose I'd better read this. Come in, please."

The Western Union guy busies himself with the coffee-bean grinder, a backing track to the syncopated words Giselle now reads.

HAD TO SAY I'M ON MY WAY—PANDRA

"Anything good?" he asks, voice raised and whiny.

"No, a client letting me know her whereabouts. Doesn't

tell me much though. I think she's being deliberately elliptical."

"Telegrams are good for that. What does she do?"

"Oh, it's not important. I'm sorry to be short, if that sounded short. But it's a long story—which is what you said yours was?"

He pours the milk into two dizzily patterned mugs, followed by dripping coffee.

"Oh, yeah. Apart from this, I also do Tupperware parties."

Giselle gasps.

"No, it's not that bad!"

"Sorry, it's just, I've heard this before. A man called Troy, I think."

"You know Troy Harder? He's a living legend in food storage."

"I don't know him, but I know of him. I know someone who's been to one of his parties."

"You mean, a party he's been at. I'm sure she was very entertained and informed. He's our highest grosser. His story's much more interesting than mine, you should probably speak to him."

He sets down his mug. "Are you a reporter or something?"

"No, well, yes, in a way. How could I get in touch with him, or you?"

"Have you got a card? Here's mine."

Giselle reads it. "*Jerry Sinclair, Various and Sundry.* Here, I'll trade you." She fetches her card: a lavishly retouched photo with blue-sky backdrop on one side; the reverse displays information in box-score format: runs, hits, no errors.

"Thanks for your time," she says.

He drains his coffee and stands to leave.

"Hey, no problem. Thanks for the coffee. I'll let myself out." Jerry does so, taking a quick dip into the Sands ashtray along the way.

At the office, Giselle decides to assume that Pandra will allow her book to be shopped and to make a sweep of publishing houses. Strood makes copies of various portions as Giselle writes letters, careful to mention that this constitutes a simultaneous submission. Whether that's taboo in the current climate is immaterial at Crazing—Giselle prides herself on making her own judgments, following her instincts as a kind of safeguard against losing her own edgy interest. Even the act of submission is outside her normal job description.

Her mind fixes on the idea of *childproofing* and she's visualizing plastic hinges on pantry doors when a call comes in from the mother of Crazing's child prodigy, Frances Culligan.

"Giselle? Whitney Culligan. Frannie, pipe down! Sorry, she's playing the organ and singing along. Sharper on that high C! Less sugar, more tart! Think Kool-Aid in reverse! Sorry, Giselle, I'm back now. It's a week to the audition—anything new?"

Giselle scans her thoughts speedily. "I haven't heard that there's anyone after the part who's as right as Frances. There's a sitcom actress but she'd have to play much younger than her years, which might not be easy. Plus I know the casting director wants an unknown who's in the ballpark age group."

"You calling my baby unknown? Frannie, don't sit on the

keys! And put the kitten down! No, I'm only joking. I don't want you to think I'm one of those stage mothers."

"Or that Frances was born in a trunk," Giselle laughs.

"What do you mean? I had her at Cedars, fourth floor. She wailed like corrugated metal when she came out. That's when I knew she'd taken after her father."

Giselle didn't reply. Whitney's husband had been a rock star whose suicide involved a noose made from guitar strings.

"Well, I just wanted to check in with ya," Whitney concludes. "Keep up the good work." She pops her Double Bubble over and over, like a 21-gun salute.

Giselle calls Strood over and instructs her to ready a story about Frances to plant, to aid her profile for the role of *Angie Baby*, a stage musical based on the Helen Reddy song. "Just think up anything, maybe involve Adon."

"But Frances has barely started school!" Violet protests.

"Oh yes, she has," retorts Giselle. "This here's the school for scandal. By the way, are you free tonight?"

"Is this a trick question?"

"Len's playing, debuting his new band at the Batten Down Bar."

"What happened to the other band?"

"Oh, it's still Highway Hypnosis, just with different people. I was hoping you'd come along with me, lend a little objectivity."

Violet exhales dramatically. "The way I feel about country music, negativity's more like it. But if you want, I'll come. I could use some rednecks and longnecks."

"And no-necks with bounced checks? Should I tell Len we've written his first hit?"

Violet Strood takes the long view of the L-shaped counter at the Batten Down Bar. She stands back, withstanding the glances of the regulars: men in split-soled work boots and padded flannel shirts.

"At least I *think* that's padding," she whispers to Giselle who, not listening, replies, "It's probably silicone."

Giselle hasn't seen Len yet, opting to leave him alone to gather his moods and then suspend them like lucky stars, the right tension being key, as when winding a music box.

Highway Hypnosis take the stage, a barely raised stoop above the concrete dance floor, and perform a signature instrumental to a distracted audience, a handful of whom cry for the jukebox to be turned on again.

But when Len appears, a hush descends, like the quiet that follows four selections for a dollar; it's as though the crowd had waited to receive a welcome warning, one that would excite and constrain them. "Good evening," he says.

"I'd say good night, since that's what it is, but I don't want you all to think you can leave yet. No, I've got something to tell you about first." He strums the opening chords to "Give Me the Chance To Say We're Through," and the band jumps in.

"I work damn near every day," he says between numbers, as if bantering while calling bingo. "What I do is this… you know Stater Brothers market?"

The crowd cheers their familiarity.

"And you know those shopping carts? Place up front for kiddies in the saddle? Well, every day, right there in the lot, I round those suckers up into a twenty-mule-team wagon train.

"Funny thing is, I can't park my own car in the lot, 'cause I might take a space away from all you customers out there. So some days it seems like I'm 'Walking Halfway from Texas.'"

The crowd listens to the song without a rustle. Even the bartenders clear glasses in slow motion. By the time Len sings "Where Were You When I Was Falling in Love?" they are as confirmed as Catholics on their fifteenth birthdays. Delirious applause like a drunken stampede sends Len off, then rip-tides him back for two encores.

Quick to rush to him backstage is bigshot manager Naylor Francis, whose connections to Nashville are as taut as his braided leather tie. He talks rapidly of his contacts at the currently infallible Destiny Records and holds out the prospect of a label deal and historic recording sessions, predicated on Len's willingness to sign up with him and then to fly, as soon as possible, to Tennessee. He fixes an appointment with Len for the next afternoon and sweeps out again.

Giselle waits for Len to emerge from the dressing room. When he finally does, he seems the same yet different, as if his soul's been tuned up. He kisses Strood's cheek while his arm's around Giselle's waist. Soon he steers her to the back door, where his car is parked. The others in Highway Hypnosis are busily loading equipment, helped by various hangers-on.

Violet waves good-bye to Giselle and Len and then walks back through the now-familiar bar, towards the front door where her own car is parked in a fenced-in lot. From this asphalt landscape she looks back at the Batten Down Bar and marvels at how Len's lodestone of experience, exquisitely romanced, has made friendly territory out of a world she had always been loathe to visit, and would once have driven through with windows tight.

At Len's cottage-style house the cement steps and river-rock foundation glisten in the moonlight like a manmade brook surrounding a condominium. His screen door is wood-framed, a *Gone Fishing* sign contradicting his welcome mat. Inside, his Adirondack chair holds a laundry basket full of shirts and underwear, and then Giselle's pocket-monogrammed shirtwaist dress. They embrace in the slicing light.

"I'm so thrilled for you," Giselle ventures, knowing her words will startle the silence in which Len is basking. He's flushed with success at a show that's gone over so well, not to mention being courted by Naylor Francis, and seemingly hopes to ride it forever, never to return to a world short on audience response. At length he squeezes her hand, pulls away from her.

"I feel like I'm conducting a séance here," she says. "Len, if you're out there, give me a sign. Shake a tambourine. Levitate a table."

He picks up a Navajo blanket to hug himself. And he stares at her.   "Sometimes I think the only thing that distinguishes lovers from other pairs is that they look at each other a little too long," he says. "But then, you and I both do work that calls for a lot of staring."

"Are you saying that since we're lost to our work, you think we're lost on each other?"

"I don't know. It's like we live too much in our brains, high up on cliffs like the Pueblo people did, or the Anasazi."

"The Anasazi disappeared without a trace, if I remember correctly," Giselle replies.

"Well, you would know. It's like you to bring up little morsels better left undisturbed." Len sits on a throw-covered sofa. "You know, I don't even know what this couch really looks like."

"But when we're not together," Giselle says, crouching to the floor and sitting on Len's pale-blue work shirt, "aren't you aware of me with you? Loving you, exasperated by you—holding you right up close and then at arm's length—but always there?"

"I suppose I might be, but I'm not sure. I don't even really want to talk about this. Do you feel the way you just said about me when I'm not around?"

Giselle worries a loose thread on a starched cuff. "If I stop to think, I guess... I guess I only feel alone."

"That's it. That's what's wrong between you and me. It's like we're one of these technically created duets by two people who are never in the same studio. One of them could even be dead. Hell, they could both be dead. And still, one dreams of singing with the other all their life, but the other person may never even know their partner exists."

"Oh, thanks a lot. You're saying I'm just some kind of doting special effect."

"I don't know what I'm saying right now."

"And could one of those duets be on your song, 'Where Were You When I Was Falling in Love?' Are you in love with someone else, and you want me out?"

"Maybe I'm in love with someone else and want you in," he replies. "I'm not—there's no one else. I just don't know."

"Well, Len, I'll give you credit for one thing. At least you didn't wait till we were in bed to break the bad news. You know what they say: bad news always happens in or near a bed." Giselle watches him weigh her words, as if assessing whether there's melody in them.

"I'm not saying we're through," he says. "I'm just saying maybe we should take a break—take five for a while. And I still want to work with you. We're a great team that way, two of a kind expanding into a full house."

Giselle, who's steadfastly refused to let emotions rule her, sighs. "I'll be in touch," she says, struggling to put a lilt in her flat voice. "Or you can call me." She puts her dress on and gathers her things. When she closes the screen door behind her, its hook latch clatters like trailing heels. She almost turns to see if it's Len, but quickly corrects her gait.

As she reaches curbside, she realizes she hasn't got her car, and it's then she cries: tears of anger at herself for letting her independence slip, and for thinking she could get around while willing herself into someone else's hands.

She'll have to call a cab. She'll have to walk back into Len's house and use the phone—no, *ask* if she can use the phone. Before knocking on the screen's wood frame she readies what she'll say.

"You always say you like it when I talk about leaving," she tells him. "Well, here I am, back."

"You can stay if you need to," Len replies.

"No, that's not a good idea. I just need to make a call." She uses the kitchen phone, judging it to be the most neutral.

"I almost laughed when you said 'Shake a tambourine,'" he tells her as she stands looking out the screen door. "When I was a kid, I swore I'd never play drums, because on slow songs I might have to play the tambourine." He laughs. "Could you see me as a drummer?"

"I can't see you at all," she answers.

Two things happen the morning after what looked like the last of the checkered cabs had collected Giselle from Len's house and away from their stand-off. First, she receives an invitation to a progressive dinner hosted by Troy Harder of Tupperware fame; next, *Monotony*, a satirical alternative to *Daily Variety*, now coming close to usurping it, prints an item about Adon babysitting for Frances Culligan. A blaze had broken out in the promissory kitty of a poker game, the story runs, and the fire department had turned up. In what amounts to a Sue Lyonization, the writer manages to take note of Frances' babydoll pajamas.

The article is read with great interest by two new arrivals from England. The Bewley Sisters, they're calling themselves here, and their aim is to abduct.

At Stater Brothers, Len is busily matchmaking carts while speculating on his imminent departure for Nashville. He half wonders who will look after Kachina, his silky terrier, now that he can't really ask Giselle.

THE BEWLEY SISTERS: Janine and Hermione

I first saw Hermione crying on a truncated train on the North London Line. I wondered who it was, this extraordinary eavesdropper (she was obviously listening to my conversation through her tears). She crossed and uncrossed her sleek ankles, leaned her plump-heeled shoes in a manner that made me long to be in love. Meanwhile my companion, Maron, kept talking to me, occasionally of chaos, fevered with the charm of one who really tries and still comes up short.

"How can you be so beautiful?" he said to me suddenly. And then the sting: "I just wish you loved me."

I didn't. I dreamed only extreme dreams, beds or roses. Having a poverty of habit, I didn't know what to do in most situations. Still, something told me to follow this girl; however briefly, she'd made her cause mine. I rode on past Kentish Town West, where Maron got off to haunt the dusty music shops. I stayed on, past everything, until the train butted to a stop in North Woolwich.

It was getting dark, but became fractionally lighter once we'd headed south, crossing the Thames on the Woolwich ferry. I was sure Hermione had noticed me now—I'd limbo'd under the dock's mechanical arm, which had dropped to signal imminent departure.

Sitting on a bench, using a porthole for a mirror, she was straining for natural light. I thought it must be all to do with the gradual weight of things. Once in Woolwich, the pedestrian district was wide, the high-street shops cheaply and artificially lit. When Hermione went into a café, I came and sat at her table. The baked potato she began to dissect seemed to sigh.

"Why were you listening to me earlier?" I challenged.

"Why have you followed me?"

"Did you hear what I was saying back there on the train? Was that why you were crying?"

"Why, no," she replied. "I was thinking about something I'd overheard on another day, 'on another floor/in the back of a car...'"

"'In the cellar of a church with the door ajar,'" I completed, and it was clear we understood one another. I went back to her flat where we dyed our hair with succulent henna. My gray bits came up brassy as a veterans' parade.

Now we were the Bewley Sisters, and we hatched a plot to kidnap David Bowie. Our ransom note would be cut-up lyrics and pages from *Junky*. The girl's name was Hermione and that made me jealous, so I lied and said mine was Janine and I came from Detroit.

We shook hands goodnight and agreed we'd go to Switzerland; we'd eat chocolate on the train that skirts Lake Geneva, then head for Vevey to be very close to what we wanted.

Soon I moved in with Hermione, at her flat in Beckenham, where I was troubled by belabored Bowie symbolism. And while I wouldn't necessarily say I bossed her around, it was no coincidence I'd been a yell-leader at my high school, the one with the mouth rather than the moves.

We never went out except to work; she was a barmaid, I was an editorial secretary for a magazine called *Heating and Plumbing News*. We stayed in nights and saved up to travel to Switzerland.

Once there, though, we had hardly any money and no language other than our own private one, based on Hermione repeating, Berlitz-style, every single idea I ever had.

We found Bowie's house in Vevey, but never got any nearer than the flower beds, from which we took dirt and blossoms as keepsakes. I pressed the flowers in plastic and they melted to look like a sheet of chocolate-flavored saltwater taffy.

We spent all of one night in Vevey, a place so alien it unnerved me. I wondered why our hero, who spoke in his songs just to us, would choose to live somewhere so devoid of emotion and empathy. I gave up on the place the next morning while eating a jam-laden roll. Hermione followed; we went on to Geneva and stayed in an old hotel we could almost afford.

The trip turned out to be more pilgrimage than plot; we made no further effort to kidnap Bowie or even get a glimpse of him. Instead, walking on a concrete trail past an ostentatious fountain, luxury jewelry shops, and repellent couture, we spoke about what we wanted from life.

But when we got back to Beckenham, all of England was no good to me anymore. I told Hermione we were going to LA, where living was dirt cheap. There she got work in an Irish pub, while I became a floater for the *Los Angeles Times*. I got sent to departments where help was needed: classifieds, accounts, subscriptions, photo library. For the first time since high school, I had to abide by a dress code.

One day I saw a copy of *Monotony*, from which the *Times* writers sometimes pinched ideas. It had an item about a useless teen idol baby-sitting child star Frances Culligan, herself the daughter of a rock star. The thing was, that child lived near us, in a Spanish stucco house crowned in security thorns of wrought iron.

I'd always found the house an oddity: with that overwrought fencing, it must have been bought some time ago, before the neighborhood's decline, and later fortressed and buttressed. Out of reach but visible were the yard's banana trees and other tropical vegetation; a silver tabby cat sometimes slunk through the bars and lounged among an array of Mexican pottery on the porch.

I hadn't realized before that the tap-dancing child I'd seen prancing down the street was famous. I thought it might be wise if I tried to befriend her. That night over fish-and-chips TV dinners, I gave Hermione the news and persuaded her that kidnapping, like desire, was a strong cocktail comprised of equal parts nonresignation and the memory of being poor, which is a thing you always have with you, rubbing up against your legs like a damp and hungry cat. I stressed that this would be kidnapping with a *kid*, that much easier, and our own Lindbergh-style ladder to the stars.

"But I thought the Lindbergh baby died," she said, before she got the point. If she ever got the point.

I sat that night and visualized my ransom notes. Maybe for this I'd cut up books by Jay McInerney to use in my communiqués—creating puns like COMMA, BABY LIVES to let the mother know her moppet was not only okay but in the care of someone with a superior sense of literary and grammatical humor.

The next morning, as I left to catch the Number 10 bus to work, I hung back a little when I saw Frances' mother pushing her child out the door. Frances skipped spiritedly down the street, the snaps on her backpack flapping. She halted, picked up a coin, skipped it into a sidewalk crack, then pounced on it with both feet.

She slid the backpack off one small, curved shoulder, opened the catch, and pulled out a case of pancake makeup, a bottle of Sun-In, and a tube of cheap claret lipstick. These things might be for Show & Tell, along with the twig from a bottle-brush tree and the slicing stalk of Pampas grass she collected as she advanced down the block.

Frances turned left to greet a bulbous yellow school bus, the awkward crossbreed of a lunch-box and a bumblebee. I stayed waiting for the Number 10, which originated in seaside Santa Monica and was an oxidized dirty blue. I decided to approach Frances when we repeated our tracing-book steps the next morning. I knew she was probably coached not to speak to strangers, but felt I might appear benign—a kid of grown-up stature, a figurine of fun in my high-top tennies and red jeans, with my collar spray of Chantilly lace.

GISELLE BURIES HERSELF in thoughts unrelated to Len, from whom she hasn't heard. Her home phone sits on its haunches and when it rings, it's Troy Harder's assistant calling to confirm Giselle's presence at his upcoming progressive dinner.

"No need to bring a covered dish," the assistant opines. "We've got the food side of things, well, *covered*. Just bring yourself, and a friend, if you like."

But Giselle plans to go alone—a friend would only emphasize Len's absence in her life. When she goes in to Crazing there's a message from Pandra, saying she's met a film producer in Mexico who's interested in her story, and would Giselle forward a copy of the manuscript to him?

Strood saunters in, wearing an orange boilersuit blazoned with *Goodyear*. Her blond hair is in twinned soap-on-a-rope braids; her large feet in jellied-plastic shoes.

"How's tricks?" she greets, and Giselle resists replying that tricks are for kids. Instead she says, "Almost as plentiful as Johns at the Cadillac Ranch."

"Well, then, how are you?"

"Not bad, Strood," Giselle pretends. "Get yourself a coffee, and we'll have a meeting to review the week ahead."

When Strood returns, Giselle is seated with a shorthand notebook balanced like a kneepad.

This week's priorities, she recites and jots. *Pandra, Tupperware/Troy Harder, Brad/VistaVision*

Second place: Sidonia Burne's cat book
Forgotten but not gone: Adon, Frances, Them Park
In Limbo: Hedda Hophead, Len Tingle

"Len Tingle?" Violet asks, aghast, then clears her throat and nods. "Len Tingle."

Giselle tries not to fix on Len, not to think of how she'd spoken to her mom over the phone about the broken relationship while trying to untangle a fistful of delicate necklaces. She looks far off, for effect, but is checked by Violet.

"Do you want me to try to get Pandra on the phone?"

"That's okay. I'll do it, Strood. Thanks anyway." Giselle taps out Pandra's beach-house hideaway number; surprisingly, Pandra picks up, archly reciting, "Gladstone 6620."

Before responding, Giselle jots a quick note about this; it's the kind of minutiae *Monotony* feeds on like plankton. "Pandra? Giselle here, Crazing."

"Hi."

"How was Mexico? I thought we should probably meet to talk about your book and what's going on with it."

"Yes, we need to do that. Quite a few things have changed. Why don't you come out this way? Pandra could meet you at the end of Coasta Pier."

"When, what time?"

"High noon?"

Giselle laughs self-consciously. The morning is bright and her schedule can be juggled effortlessly; only the aftermath will grate like rusty wind chimes. Giselle firms the arrangement. "See you later, then. And do not forsake me."

"What?"

"I'll see you at noon," she concludes, wishing she'd worn more fashionable shoes.

As Giselle skirts the apron coast toward Point Mugu, the Glee Club's Tammy sits cooling her plastic-and-glitter heels in Crazing's postage stamp of a waiting room. She pours herself a paper thimbleful of Arrowhead water and returns to the orange Naugahyde seat, propping her feet once again in tasteless proximity to the water-cooler spout.

Tammy's come armed with her solo effort—her first away from Glee Club—a dancey croon she's called "Shinola." Violet, unsure what to do with the pulsating, gum-popping miscreant before her, excuses herself to call Giselle on the car phone.

"It's me," Violet says in a conspiratorial voice. She knows the walls have acoustically aided ears. "I've got one of the Glee Club here."

"You must mean Hedda Hophead. I don't think any of the Glee Club know where our office is."

"This one does. She's called Tammy."

"Uh-oh. Whatever she wants, make out like you're giving it to her. What *does* she want, anyway?"

"She's got a tape, a solo tape."

"A *what* tape? I can't hear you."

"Solo."

"That was quick. Well, give it a listen with her there, see what you think, and then tell me about it later—when I'm back and she's gone."

"Okay, chief." Violet hangs up and motions Tammy into a cubicle with a stereo. Tammy reaches into her clear vinyl shopping bag for a cassette with an '84 Olympics color scheme, and pops it into the player. "Shinola" unwinds, the twisted tale of a romantic triangle syncopated by a busy signal. The singer, a temporarily jilted Jolene, triumphs over her wayward lover:

he's powerless to belong to anyone else. When he returns, she incants, his tail is yet another thing between his legs.

Strood finds it hard to keep a smile at bay; trying to do so, she ends up smirking like a thumbnail outhouse moon.

As Len drives toward Crazing, he thinks about a commercial he saw on late-night television: a stick figure of a man wandering through his Carpet Kingdom, bellowing the merits of his shag-piled domain. His staff was a carpet beater; as he used it to make puns about his low, low prices he shouted at intervals, "I *am* the king!" It's not the braggadocio but the emphasis that stays with Len, as if the Carpet King needed to remind himself of who he was, in case he forgot and thought he drove a bus.

Len hums along to what music he finds on the car's AM radio, which only functions when the car goes over a bump in the road. "I *am* the king," he ad-libs and syncopates, evoking the surrey with the fringe on the top.

It takes Violet a few moments to recognize Len on the stucco front steps, which wink and melt like candy coins in the hot sun. The gold threads of his Western shirt shimmer, too, as if flirting with the ground. Violet, in the elaborate process of showing Tammy out, greets Len and feels obliged to let slip that Giselle is out.

But Len just looks at Tammy, unable to summon the breath for a hello. He's smacked by her presence, her fearlessness and elegance. Tammy's view of Len is that he has the warm, open face of an aging teen idol, the tugboat weight of years providing their own glamour assist. "Have I met you?" she asks.

"No, I don't think so," Len replies, introducing himself.

"Well, I'm Tammy Whynot."

"Why not accompany me for some lunch?" Len asks and they depart without even a good-bye to Violet. They go to the Mainliner Diner where Tammy orders a piece of Sedgwick pie. She reaches into her armadillo handbag, decapitating the petrified creature in the process. She smoothes her Indian Princess dress, its ribbed fabric a rough, ridge-riding crepe. She lights a long cigarette, a woman's brand she'd been loyal to ever since it was launched in her infancy. "A silly millimeter longer" she intones to her soft drink's twisty straw.

And Len keeps staring, looking at Tammy's baby face, her chubby arms, while thinking of Giselle. *Where were you when I was falling in love?"* he asks silently, knowing now what his song had tried to foreshadow.

"I don't smoke," he replies to the offered slender cigarette. "Anyway, I'd feel naked smoking that without a cigarette holder." And he shivers at having uttered two words he'd like to apply to Tammy: naked, hold her.

"Because it fucks up your voice?" she asks, jolting Len. He notices that while Tammy polishes her fingernails, unlike Giselle she does not do her toes. He asks her about it.

"It's a good rule of thumb," she says. "Never go out with anyone who paints their toenails." Then it is as if Len has christened her bowed hair with a bottle of champagne, as Tammy, moving away from him slightly, launches into her story.

"I never seemed to have time for Elvis the way other people did," she explains. "The same with James Dean, Jean Harlow, Valentino, Vicious. It's like they belonged so much to their time—and the time just after it—that they gave up being timeless. They were not for me. I liked Andy Warhol. I thought he was different. He was as starstruck as a sequined jacket and his myth got bigger until he died. Then he was like a palooka."

Tammy pauses. "Or is palooka a kind of bubble gum?" Gum has misled her before: stuck bits in the street flattened so they resembled the plectrums her old boyfriend was always in need of, since he was constantly losing them through the floor-boards of their creaky apartment. "The mice around here must have a helluva band," he'd say, and the dog would bark.

"I used to live with this guy," she continues telling Len, "and all the while I was collecting my Warhol stuff. But one day I moved out, came west via rest areas and Route 69—if you get my drift—and eventually got to La Milagra where I met Hedda and her gang. For a long time I missed the stuff I'd dumped, but by then I had a sideline in refrigerator art, which I sold at the Orange Drive-In swap meet. Magnets, you know, and shit like that. I decided it was pretty Warholian and that my days as a fan were over. I don't collect any more, and I don't care.

"But since Hedda was putting together this band, Glee Club Mark Two, I thought I might as well join. But what I'm really into is duets, songs like 'Lucky Stars,' with that line 'I might not be all that bright/but I know how to hold you tight'; and songs that have a story, like 'Copacabana' and the Pina Colada song."

"What about a song like 'Somethin' Stupid'?" Len interjects.

"It's okay, but I'm not through yet. I'm just trying to say the Glee Club isn't really for me... but don't repeat that."

"What is?" Len asks. "What is for you?"

"I'm getting to that. As I said, duets and stories. Country music's okay but I like more of a highbrow... I mean, a hybrid."

"Is that anything like a highball?"

When Tammy smiles, Len knows he's cracked it.

In Len's bed, Tammy plays with Kachina, the terrier. Over martinis and gimlets in the Happy Hospital, Len had told her all the things he longed to do to her. At his home, however, none of it materialized: he seemed unable to put his mouth where his mouth was.

So Tammy sits up, a sheet draped across her chest like a ball gown, and plays fetch with Kachina, who retrieves a tennis ball not much smaller than her skull. She's silently thankful for Len's nonperformance, not caring much for sex; particularly its attendant sounds, which remind her of soggy huaraches, sandals not designed with inclement weather in mind.

At the progressive dinner, Giselle looks over the appetizers: the festive spurt of Cheez-Whiz filling rafts of celery, plastic gunboats of onion dip awaiting the diving-board plunge of cut carrots. But neither the food in its impressive array of containers nor the impending arrival of Troy Harder entices her. Instead she replays Pandra at the end of Coasta Pier, looking chic in bell-bottoms, a vaguely naval shirt, and red espadrilles that snaked up her legs like ties around shapely masts.

Pandra had straightened her comically tilted sunglasses, then fixed her level gaze on Giselle. "First off," Pandra said, advancing, "let me say that Pandra has an idea where the body might be buried, so to speak."

"Is that cryptic or triptych?" Giselle quipped. "Another puzzle or a kind of panel game?"

"I see wit, rather than wardrobe, is still your strong suit. Let's get a drink, shall we?"

Over coffee in institutional Melmac cups, Pandra clarified. "The body in Pandra's memoir. Except now I'm not so sure there is a body."

"I don't follow."

"Pandra met an old friend while she was in Mexico who swears she's seen Rory Otis down there, in Oaxaca."

"If that were true, then you couldn't very well have killed him, could you?"

"I know. But I'm really not sure. That would mean Perry..." she trailed off.

After a minute or so she picked up again. "As Pandra said in her message to you, she met a guy in Mexico who's serious about the film rights to her story. Reese says he checks out. Pandra had been thinking that a murder mystery would lend a human-interest, uh, hand. A hook. But solving another kind of mystery might be even better."

"Pandra, how on earth do you want to play this?"

"Highest bidder for the book, film in production, publicized scavenger hunt for Rory, dead or alive."

"But a scavenger hunt is about collecting useless things."

"I'd forgotten you're so literal," Pandra said.

"Still I like the sound," Giselle continued.

"Great, isn't it? Kind of old-fashioned, like a progressive dinner," Pandra had said, while Giselle felt the draft of synchronicity, the shadow of someone stepping over the shallowest of graves.

At the dinner party, Giselle tries to find out about Vicki Prescott, the artist whose career she'd backburnered. In front of a fondue pot, momentarily daunted by the tiny prong she holds in her hand, Giselle receives a reply from a woman called Candida.

"I got a postcard from Vic a while back," she says. "It had giant jackrabbits on it, so I figured she was probably doing all right in the romance department."

Giselle nods, then heads for her arranged place at one of several card tables. Scrutinizing a centerpiece made from sculpted balloons, Giselle worries again that Pandra's story doesn't add up. She wonders if maybe she's only envious, or feels diminished when she's around Pandra.

Soon the table fills with several decades' worth of women, the youngest one barely eligible to vote. It might be all she'll ever stretch to, Giselle reflects: putting an x on a piece of paper. She's alarmed by her venomous thoughts. Or is she green with envy, certain this is the young woman Len has left her for?

To her left, an elegant older lady named Barbara—not Barbie, she laughs—begins to extol Tupperware's three-in-one freezer set. "It's remarkable how they nest," she assures Giselle. "Why, when you're not using them, they seem to take up no room at all."

Giselle keeps thinking of Len. At length she realizes she must say something by way of polite conversation. "Do you still have to burp them?" she asks, retrieving from memory an item of Tupperware protocol.

Barbara toys with her bracelet; it tinkles like high-octave piano keys against the anemic stemware. "Why, yes, I think it's recommended."

"That's the best part," says the final quarter of their table, a tiny brunette whose name is Shari. "Of course we've been trying for a baby so..."

"So this is the next best thing?" Giselle asks, intrigued.

"Better!" Barbara laughs.

The hostess taps her daughter's battery-operated microphone, which resembles a toucan, and begins to speak. "Ladies, welcome to my home and the sixth in our series of progressive dinners. Now, some of you may wonder where we're going next, since that's what a progressive dinner is. The short answer is: nowhere, tonight. The 'progress' refers to two things. One, where we'll be next month—Alice Shue's, by the way—and secondly, the revolution in styles and the scientific advances we see available to us each month when we gather.

"Those of you who are first-timers, and I know there are a few—you'll soon see that each time we get together, there's a new freezer pack or lunchbox addition that's so improved you feel you can't get by without it. Of course, we're not fifties housewives any more, concerned with little more than martinis and Martinizing..."

Giselle takes this in, considers her own predilection for Sanforized jeans and snap-button blouses.

"But we're women of the next century: busy, whole, influential, good friends. These plastic companions free us up for other things and represent progress, the way Post-It Notes took over from clumsy refrigerator boards, where the Magic Marker message always ended up dripping like some kind of plasma..."

She's good, thinks Giselle. This is better than a night at the theater.

"You'll hear about this month's item in a moment, but first

I know you're all waiting for Troy Harder."

Troy enters stage right—from what's really a spare bedroom—and waves off the premature applause. His smile is bright; his slacks, permaprest. He looks as though he was born bronzed.

"Thanks, Ginny."

He turns to his audience. "I asked Ginny not to give me much of an introduction because I wanted to start by pointing out that buildup is really an enemy. Waxy, yellow—you don't want it on your floors, your teeth... or your Tupperware."

Giselle retrieves her Chinette napkin, which has fallen to the floor, reflecting that Troy is too old, no replacement for Adon's encroaching-goatee era.

"Hey, you, duck and dive!" Troy calls to Giselle. "How 'bout coming up here and being my Carol Merrill?"

Giselle rises to the challenge and heads for the dais.

"And what's your appellation?"

"Giselle," she giggles, as if she'd been asked her favorite tipple.

"Okay, Gazelle, why not leap over here and man my easel. Ginny, dim the lights!" As the overhead lamps are lowered, two track floodlights illuminate Troy and his assistant at the upright hobby horse.

"I began life in 1960, which was the Playtex bust of the baby boom," he says. "Turn, please."

Giselle flips a manila page. A schoolyard is depicted.

"Behold, Clark N. Dye grade school. Me, Mr. Forgettable. No glasses to be called four-eyes, no athletic ability to be a jock. Not enough gray matter to be Einstein, and I'm not talking about the hair.

"Then one day I forgot my lunch. Enter my mom, into

the school cafeteria. The entire congregated first lunch saw me called to the stage and presented with a perfect specimen, a lunch so immaculately, so elaborately packed it looked like a station wagon prepared for a cross-country trip. From that day on I was Troy Tupperware, Tupper for short. Turn, please."

Giselle misses a beat, thinking this is another part of his name.

"High school. Mid-1970s. Me, Junior President, running for spring election on the presidential ticket. I win, take the results home to my dad. He leaves me a note with my next day's lunch—yes, I'm still taking it. The note reads *Next time try harder*. In that moment, I don't get mad and I don't get hurt. Instead I know my life's calling, I know that Tupperware is to be my life's work. Turn, please.

"The vast array of foodware you see here has never failed to uplift or inspire me. Unlike my two marriages, a sports car, or a flutter on the market, these sturdy containers are trustworthy; reliable; awe-inspiring. You may have heard of Toastmasters. I'm proud to say you're looking at a Tupperware Master, an honor which, I have to say, humbles me.

"Now, I know you're all waiting for this month's addition. Turn. Remember I began by talking about buildup? What's in this tiny spray bottle eradicates all that at the touch of a fingertip. So year after year, day after day, your Tupperware can look the way it did the first time you took it out of the shrink-wrap, before it ever had a close encounter with a sink. It's $9.95, refillable, of course, and cheap at thrice the price. The fountain of youth in a bottle. If only we could make that as a face cream, we'd let Avon know!"

"You don't need it, Troy," Barbara calls, clearly a plant.

"Shucks," he replies, to voluminous applause as the entrées are brought in.

Len sits on the balcony, a coffin-sized ledge of concrete fixed to the back of his new Highland Park apartment. He looks over the tenants' parking spaces as if they were his personal spread. His gaze dwells on his Datsun pickup—too old to be a Nissan, too flimsy for a Ford. Yet the truck is all he's got: his furniture, save for his hillbilly Adirondack chair, is rented; the TV borrowed.

"Everything I own is in the back yard," he sighs. "Everything I owe is inside." He comes back inside, past a leaning, sliding glass door that has come off its track, and picks up his audio recorder to preserve the words. The cigarette pack–size machine is serving as a paperweight for his ticket to Nashville the next morning.

Hearing her master's voice, Kachina lifts her head from his abandoned plaid slipper and goes to him. She follows Len to the hall closet where he takes down a shapeless garment bag. As Kachina realizes Len is packing to leave, she lowers her head again.

"There now, girl," Len says. "Mr. Kachina will be back and better than ever. He'll keep you in Alpo, get you that Hi-Pro Glow for the rest of your dog years. So don't go picking a Milk Bone with me." He picks up the little dog, who licks his cheek and the corner of his slightly downturned mouth.

Reviewing the Tupperware evening beside a nesting tower of plastic, Giselle adjusts the containers and herself on the sofa. As her thoughts lunge toward Len, she wonders why the view from the loveseat is always the same.

Earlier in the day, word had come of Len's imminent departure for Nashville with his new manager. She must liaise with him before he goes, and is set to do so at a coffee shop, chimingly called Hashville, where the freeways meet the runways in Westchester.

Hashville's immodest sign breaks the gray Los Angeles morning like a sandwich board. The coffee shop's sticky, depressing interior does little to lift Giselle's spirits. She pours a thimbleful of milk into a cup of coffee. Recalling Len's habit of ordering in diner-ese, she contemplates asking for "Adam and Eve on a raft" without a hint of nostalgic affectation.

Her waitress approaches, carrying a creamer in the shape of a cow. "Careful with this," the woman orders. "It's filled with sugar—not cream. We had cream but it kept clotting up and choking the cow." She tilts the vessel to demonstrate. "See? No dice."

"Don't people get mixed up?" Giselle feels justified in asking.

"Sometimes. But most of our clientele, they're either asleep or dead or high, or unscrewing the top of a saltshakers so an avalanche comes out. Salt mines. Still, that's my life." She hands Giselle a smudgy menu and walks off, forgetting to top up a wanting cup of coffee.

Len enters through the exit door, managing to look windswept in the airless conditions. He sits kitty-corner to Giselle in the booth after kissing her left temple. Then he puts his hand down the back of her neck, where he adjusts the tag peeking over the top of her collar.

Giselle pulls away. "I hate it when you do that," she bites. "Makes me feel like you're always correcting me. You don't see me adjusting you, do you? Not that I couldn't. And did I ever complain about things like your socks—the ones with the colored toes and heels—the ones little old ladies use to make toy monkeys, with buttons for eyes?"

"Are you through yet?"

"And I want some more coffee, though why I don't know."

"Excuse me," Len says to the waitress who arrives with what appears to be a fresh pot of coffee.

"Your magic touch again," Giselle concedes.

"What was that?"

"Nothing, nothing. Where were we? Oh yes, Nashville. Keep me posted, faxed, will you? What's your first day like?"

"Naylor has set up a couple of meetings. And lunch. Don't worry, I won't sign anything without reading it first. I won't give away my publishing rights or buy the Brooklyn Bridge."

"Len, don't condescend to me and I won't do it to you, either. Business, you know. Sorry. By the way, who's looking after Kachina?"

"That's one thing I was going to tell you. Little girl you know."

"Frances Culligan?" Giselle asks, outraged.

"No, no. Tammy. Glee Club girl."

"I see." Giselle looks at Len's somewhat sheepish face. "Have some cream for your coffee, Len. Why don't you use this cute little creamer?"

As he upends the miniature plastic cow, the sweetener he detests snowflakes into his cup. "Shh-sugar!"

Giselle laughs and excuses herself to the ladies' room. During her absence, Len loosens the silver dome of a salt-shaker.

Their oblong plates arrive. As Giselle moves to season her eggs over easy, Len grabs her wrist and wrests the shaker from her. Deftly he tightens the lid.

"Always the hero," Giselle says, and the two stare at each other disappointedly, like two lovers who've finally met, but only at the tail end of their respective good looks. They sit in silence for the remainder of the meal, until Giselle drops Troy's name, a kind of tat for Tammy's tit, and Len flinches. He grabs the check, and as they leave knocks over a grubby pitcher of boysenberry syrup. To cover his embarrassment he buys a dozen individually wrapped chocolate mints from a monkey-pod bowl next to the cash register.

About the time Len is asking a Nashville waiter to "drag one through Georgia," that is, add chocolate syrup to his Coca-Cola (he almost gets thrown out), Giselle is sitting in the Ferne Bar, listening to Troy evaluate his brunch. She is so bored, so isolated she feels it to her soul's wick. Still, she smiles and nods at the appropriate places, sure that the best way to tend to her trampled heart is to distract it.

She's not sure there is much she wants to do for Tupperware Troy in terms of his career, where he already appears to be at the top of his game. Between munches peppered with ponderous diatribes about things like vegetable crispers, Troy mentions infomercials and home shopping with all the grip and tenacity of a nouveau magnate.

"Sounds good," Giselle answers, she's not sure to what. She's wondering what it will be like to be his girlfriend—whether she'll be expected to answer his knock at the door clothed in a Saran Wrap sarong.

"Gee, you're really great," he says, apropos of nothing Giselle can assess. "My last ex-wife would never let me bend her ear like this. How come you're single?"

She pictures herself as an individually wrapped slice of processed cheese, packed tightly against identical others.

"I'm only just single," she replies. "Only just split up. I'm new to this game."

"Lucky for me," Troy replies. "Are you free for dinner tonight?"

"Not tonight," she fibs. "Later in the week looks okay." She looks into Troy's eyes, which glint like cats' in headlights. When she looks at him side-on, however, their finish is no more lustrous than a rubber doormat.

As they get up, he embraces her, and his hug holds the memory of high school: Troy, captain of the football team. He's like the boy in the Mystery Date board game—the guy the plastic door-latch never catches on; too quick-footed and handsome to be on the porch, he can be found only on the heroic receiving end of a Hail Mary pass. (In reality, the nearest Troy ever got to a football field was the locker cage of the gym. That was the vantage point from which he passed out towels to the boys, who then slapped one another with them as Troy cowered.)

So Giselle and Troy start going out, become an item. For

Giselle, her emotions rubbed raw, he soothes her like rosin on a bow. To Troy, Giselle is as compelling as a single ambition and she quietly sparkles like a sliver of party tinsel in a torrential downpour of colored balloons.

Len, deep in Nashville, has finished a consummate rendering of "Where Were You When I Was Falling in Love?" He updates Giselle on his progress via fax, $3 a page from his hotel lobby; but he calls Tammy, who's house-sitting Kachina, and plays her the tape over the line.

Tammy whoops and stamps her spike-heeled feet (Kachina yipping in shared excitement). "Len, you've done it!" Tammy shouts, as if this were a turn-of-the-century trunk call. "When's it coming out?"

"I'm ready to roll, but Destiny waits," Len says, repeating word for word his fax to Giselle. "But never mind me, how's my rickrack and roll girl?"

"Shit, I'm okay. We're recording, Glee Club is, but Hedda's just so damn domineering. She thinks she's Colonel Tom Parker or something."

"Machiavelli?"

"Yellow-belly! I wish I could get her to back off; that I could find her, what do you call it, aching heel? I just don't like the direction she pushes us in. I think, I think I may have gone country."

Len doesn't answer immediately, retuning his image of Tammy from a rock girl to a country singer, passing through several static stations along the way. He is curious to ask if Giselle has advised her, but can't bring himself to utter her name.

"I've been thinking, Len," Tammy continues, throwing a red rubber ball towards the kitchen to deflect Kachina's attention from her master's voice over the receiver. "Maybe we could record together, a duet."

"Hmm. Could be." Len takes care, knowing an abrupt answer could alienate Tammy and leave Kachina to face an empty bowl. "Duet, huh? Yeah, let's do it!" he enthuses.

"I even have a song picked out—that '70s one by Dean Friedman: 'Lucky Stars.' It's got great lyrics—'You can thank your lucky stars that we're not as smart as we like to think we are,'" Tammy sings, affecting a ludicrous ukulele twang.

Hedda Hophead has scored a contract for Glee Club with nippy independent label Cosmic Waxhead, and to celebrate the completion of their debut EP, *Refreshments Are Available from the Snack Bar*, the band will be playing at Adon's eighteenth-birthday bash. In terms of high profile, it's tantamount to Rushmore. The press will be there; the priority buzz an aural avalanche, an atmospheric pea-souper. Giselle and Strood are busily preparing, paying little heed to the comestibles, which are left in the capable hands of Troy.

The party's theme is Keg and Skeg, beer suds and surfboard fins. Crazing's full roster is set to attend, pending Len's westward return from Nashville, a recording contract with Destiny in his hamfists. On his flight home, languishing in business class, "the surrey with fringe benefits," as Len calls it, the attendant asks him if he'd like smoked salmon or chicken à la king for lunch.

It's his first chance to be an expense-account recording star, and he's readied his reply. "I want a radio sandwich and a doctor, hold the hail."

"I'm sorry, sir," the air hostess replies. "If you required a special meal, you had to ask for it in advance."

"I did, ma'am. I asked for a tuna sandwich and a Dr. Pepper without ice."

The woman sighs. "I'll double-check your request against your seat assignment." She storms off, leaving behind her own kind of turbulence. Moments later, she returns carrying a paper bag in her fingers, outstretched as if they were tongs. Len apologizes for causing any confusion, but the woman can't come close to forgiving him.

From atop a plump, padded bedspread, its machine-stitched rough-diamond pattern puckering like an unwanted kiss, Giselle looks around Troy's master bedroom: mirrors for sliding closet doors, his own upstairs refrigerator. A master remote control is affixed to his bedside table, hotel style. She hears Troy in the adjacent bathroom where a timed Mr. Coffee is mounted on a shelf just above the nearest double sink. He stirs the cups elaborately and loudly, and the sound echoes in Giselle's hungover head.

"For God's sake, Troy," Giselle complains, "you handle the cup as though you were the Bell of St Mark."

"And you're the belle of the ball," he grins, rounding the corner and flashing his bone-china teeth. She surveys herself in the triptych mirror: she's pallid, clammy, with ribbed shell skin, and sunken eyes. As she dons a torn black kimono she sighs. "More Bela Lugosi than belle of the ball, I think, really, Troy."

Giselle recalls the previous night, when she'd drunk too

much in order to feel too little, especially for their sex scene. The alcohol had done its job at the time, but in its usual broken-pact fashion it's now double-dealt her so that she feels every nuance: the hospital corners on the sheets, the shag-pile carpet blow-dried in one perfect direction, Troy's hapless tales of bullied school days confessed from the monogrammed pillowcase just touching hers.

"I wasn't a nerd so much as a *dren*," he'd told her.

"I don't get you."

"Don't you remember that *Happy Days* episode when Potsie talks about being a dren? Get it? Nerd spelled backwards?"

In the darkness, Giselle had grimaced. Troy was worse than she'd thought.

Back in his Los Angeles apartment, Len coasts on his new label's assurance of an upcoming hit record and an impending support slot at the Swing Auditorium. With Tammy, at present tickling his toes with a detachable marabou collar, he acts like an ingenue: impossible to trap, impossible not to pursue. He reflects on his newfound nonchalance, in prominent evidence when he's with Tammy. No more does he trip or endure death-defying pratfalls, as he was prone to in Giselle's company.

"I'm just trying to work out what to wear to the party tonight," he hears Tammy saying. "It's between a raw silk muumuu and a string bikini." She leans across the bed to retrieve Adon's invitation from its place on the floor, perilously close to the wicker wastepaper basket.

But Len doesn't answer immediately; he's thinking about

Giselle's new press release for Highway Hypnosis. Like a chain letter, her words are difficult to ignore, promising and threatening all in one staccato barred and staffed page. She blends semaphore with metaphor, and her words both alert and evoke. Len longs not to love her.

"Anything will be fine," he answers and Tammy pouts, wanting him to linger on her string-and-crochet bikini.

In the supermarket where she's collecting next-to-last-minute party supplies, Giselle is eavesdropping on a curious pair just ahead of her in line. The woman, hennaed and quietly venomous, is talking to a diminutive man.

"She thinks she murdered someone in her past," Xenia says. "I didn't actually see it, but listen, I'm no priest," she suddenly adopts the tone of the confessional, "I don't have the seal of confidentiality or anything... I'm still thinking I ought to go to the police."

"I'm not too sure about that," says the tiny man who is pairing double coupons and cleaning his nails on cardboard boxtop edges. "You may find the statute of liberty's run out on them, if it was a while ago like you say."

Xenia looks away as her Honey Nut Cheerios are being scanned, to meet Giselle's visage, eyes and mouth agape. Giselle thinks fast.

"Excuse me, but I think these are yours." She passes a long package of assorted sugared cereals over the rubber separator like a baton over a finish line.

"Thank you," says Xenia. "I shouldn't have overlooked them."

"Well, you'd have to be psychic to keep track of all your items."

"Oddly enough, that's what I am," says Xenia, and Giselle gasps theatrically.

Then she enthuses. "I'm a personal manager, a kind of modern-day talent agent, and I've been looking for someone like you! Do you have a card?"

Xenia is by now holding one, in the same hand as her scrolled shopping receipt.

"Thank you. Say, would you be interested in coming to a party?" Giselle rummages in her patent bag to produce an invite to Adon's Keg and Skeg party, which Xenia guardedly accepts.

As Giselle loads the groceries into her hatchback, she slows down and considers the party. Her clients are doing well—Frances Culligan, Adon, and Glee Club have all had successes; and Len's new record is set for a billboard on the Hollywood end of Sunset Boulevard. Not the Strip, shabbier than that—but not bad either. The board will duplicate the album's cover: a row of telephone poles with Len in a line-man's nest, the catbird seat of the album's title.

The thought of Len gives Giselle a twinge of sorrow for whatever it was they had, and she tries to look at it clinically, to surmise he loved her in theory if not in practice. Defiantly, his single comes over the radio, country station K-FROG, an Inland Empire frequency that usually fades before downtown. She listens to his voice, a steel guitar played from railway ties, an oak-aged whine: "I saw your love on a window shade tonight," he begins. "Where were you when I was falling in love?"

Giselle turns the corner and the resistant radio knob at the same time.

Adon digs out the keys to his West Hollywood condo, putting down his luggage to open the door. The baggage, heavy '70s Samsonite, plays off his simian good looks in a nod to a once-popular commercial. Or so a scandal sheet had noted, when they caught him at the airport gesturing and fumbling as he upended and hefted the weighty suitcases from the pinwheel-hypnotic conveyor belt.

Dropping his bags in his mock-marble foyer, Adon gravitates to his answering machine, which barks back gruff messages of abuse interspersed with the squeal of a bubble gum–stuck preteen and then some boasting about a job: it's like his own private version of *Snow White and the Seven Dwarfs*. He sighs in dismay—he'll have to have his phone number changed again.

Adon isn't the kind of two-faced teen idol who supplements his tidy public image with a decadent underbelly, like a redneck paunch cascading over his virile washboard-and-corncob hillbilly physique. He is a sincere if somewhat simple young man in possession of a talent that, were it an illegal substance, would fail to get him arrested.

He enjoys his fame, save for the dark side: the nasty calls, defaced posters, and taunts from the press and the public, too, who seem to resent him the same way they hate their commutes to work each morning. Adon knows he is short on credibility; but he never set out to be Bob Dylan, so why should he be bullied for it?

He was an emancipated minor and now he's independently rich at eighteen. His strong chin is covered by a fledgling but defiant goatee. Giselle has spoken to him about it, reminding him his fan base is young and pleased with him just as he is: nonthreatening and safe, a board-game marker come to life.

Len opens his back door to a bale of cold air, solid as ice and eerily unseasonable for spring in southern California. It gives him a shiver that in turn gives him a conscience that answers to the name of Giselle. For the most part, his morals are like a cryptogram, a blinking neon sign he's half-interested in completing, the way one does crosswords—to compensate, to fill a vacuum.

He walks into the kitchen, where he looks out of a small, smudgy window and visualizes seeing Giselle at that kid Adon's party tonight. Maybe he should tell Tammy he'd prefer to go alone, but that would mean he'd run the risk of Giselle turning up with Mr. Food Container. Len laughs: his ex-girlfriend has seen the future and it's airtight plastic.

Or could a person see the future? He'd had his palm read once, years ago at a carnival midway. The woman who'd done the reading, a real character, was later revealed to be a man during a police raid to get the troupe moved on. But she had pointed out a cushioned box at the base of Len's thumb: a box, she'd said, which denoted fame—its corners, its trappings, its protected space.

Len had liked that. Now he sits down at his marbled kitchen table, whose formica surface is enough like linoleum to remind himself he's hit the floor before. On cue Kachina comes in, looking from her empty water bowl to Len in a comic doubletake.

Caterers are beginning to arrive at Adon's condo, and he has to stop himself unskinny-dipping into the bowls of snacks. He thinks back to a time when his weight was more of a worry: in the days when he was a preteen, he was so pale and brittle he looked like a walking cuttlebone whittled away by a parrot. He beefed up after he began competing in skateboard contests: the extra pounds perversely buoyed him in performing intricate, airborne 360s. That heaviness helped him become a teen idol, too—made him looked filled out, as if someone had colored him in.

He loves his success as much as he hates some of the trappings—like the teen magazines with cover stories like "Would Adon Date You Twice?" and "Why Adon is Girl Shy." The serious press was even worse; a typical article began, "Adon is a pathetic creature. His fame is wide and undeserved."

It seems the only time he feels really comfortable and happy is when he walks by a restaurant with a plate-glass front. He can see the diners recognize him; they point and gesticulate, yet he can't hear what they're saying. That way, he still has a chance.

Adon recalls a story in the trade press—something about a fire breaking out when he was babysitting for his Crazing stablemate, Frances Culligan. The event was entirely fabricated—and evidently flame-retardant, since it quickly blew over. Frances will be at his party tonight and he knows, in the lingo of his upcoming film, *Summer Stock*, that she's sweet on him—probably less to do with his head on her pillow than his place on the magazine covers.

The summer theme of the party seems grossly misplaced: the day is shaping up to be irrationally cold. Tiny snowflakes fall, melting before they hit the pool deck. Still, for a moment it looks as if they might slice through the hanging fishnets filled with shells, starfish, and colored glass bowls.

It isn't Frances who interests Adon, but her mother, Whitney, who has skin and hair the color of most computer terminals. Hard Whitney, who'd never give Adon the time of day, let alone a place on her dance card. Adon sighs: this *Summer Stock* business is getting to him, he can't stop thinking in character. He steadies himself. No, no way will he ever get Whitney to go to bed with him, conscious as she is of her widowhood.

The doorbell sounds—it's a tape of a Martin Denny toucan caw, maraca-like beaks clanging like *Summer Stock*'s clapperboards. He slides the peephole (a thumbnail-size surfboard) to one side and sees Giselle with some model-type guy who looks like he's wearing a plastic wig of blond hair.

"The poultry's a bit paltry," he hears the guy saying. It must be his idea of a pun. Adon opens the door.

"At least it's not the Golden Arches," he retorts. Met with a slate-blank stare he adds, "That's what I call McDonald's."

Giselle steps in. "Troy, I'd like you to meet Adon."

"I recognize you from your posters."

"You mean there are some that aren't defaced? I'm shocked—I'm usually wearing glasses and a scribbly moustache. That's if they're being kind." Adon sighs. "Sure wish I could catch someone in the act, marking one up."

"You mean be the fly on the flyposter wall," says Giselle. "By the way, Adon, does this mean you're giving up the idea of growing a goatee?"

"I don't know," he replies, brushing his white corduroy

jeans and then his chin with a heavily ringed hand. "I think beards look kinda unkempt, and you know me—if I get dirty, I have to go home and change." He laughs nervously, having thought his goatee more successful than it evidently was, and looks out the window to see Frances Culligan approaching, two feet ahead of Whitney.

"Come on, Mother," Frances says, stamping her court shoes which match her sober blue sailor suit. In her yellow petticoat, a pineapple-upside-down cupcake holder, Whitney squats to buckle her Mary Janes. She wears a matching yellow ribbon at her throat. Frances wonders whether her mother's head would tumble off if she removed it.

"You two are early," greets Giselle, extending her right hand in vain.

"Frances has to run through her number, and I want to make sure the acoustics are right," Whitney announces from her place on her self-made tuffet.

"Is she doing 'Childproofing'?"

"I can answer for myself," replies Frances. "Since you ask, yes I am. It's the showstopper from my new play, *Angie Baby*, isn't it, Mother? In the key of C."

"I'm happy to provide some backup if you want," says Adon.

"Forget it," replies Frances. "Don't you think I know better than to ever work with pets or teen idols?"

Adon starts to walk away and Troy heads for the kitchen to oversee the preparations. "The party's due to begin at sunset," Giselle announces in a stage whisper that begs for a curtain call.

Adon, turning on his heels in the hallway, prepares to approach Whitney; he practices the line he'll use. "Are you the mother or the daughter?" he mimes, scrutinizing her imaginary hand. He thinks better of this approach. That Whitney could be Frances' sister is more plausible. He walks toward Whitney, every step an awkward leap. "How long has your sister been acting?" he ventures.

Whitney's eyes focus, a frigid blue. "My daughter, pipsqueak. And I can assure you she acted her way right out of my womb."

Adon freezes in his gangly position. His flattery has run into a flatbed truckload of block ice.

Sidonia Burne, cat author, stands with her thumbs through her copper-mesh belt. The tiny bells that hang from it tinkle as she emphasizes a point, which she does now to screenwriter Brad. "What cats want from us is the assurance that each day will be exactly like the one before."

Overhearing, Frances Culligan pauses. That sounds exactly like her late father, who was the very emblem of the word "habitual."

Across the sunken living room, Violet Strood holds a drink. "Troy is a cute little number, by the way," she says to her boss.

"Right," Giselle replies. "Just the thing to keep me cold at night." A bit drunk already on the keg beer, she responds to Violet's reproachful gaze: "I've only had two A&W mugfuls!"

As if reading a crib sheet, Len walks in, bumping the edge of a card table and causing a melon ball to wobble like a segmented, orbiting planet. He sees Giselle first of all, and everyone else takes on the appearance of a movie-musical backdrop: they are vivid but ultimately lifeless. Len knows he loves her, but must ignore this, and it undoes him.

Giselle turns away from him, her long dress a conducted orchestra of organza and she heads upstairs to retrieve a velvet wrap from Adon's queen-sized bed. For late summer it is unfathomably cold; she deep-sixes a shudder, masking it with sudden movements to suggest vibrancy. She mentally loosens her corset to more of a good-time girdle. Re-entering the party, she assesses who needs rescuing.

Adon and Whitney are at odds, but Whitney can amply take care of herself. Sidonia and Brad still huddle; Troy buzzes through his act like a bee under a tent of picnic cheesecloth. Len, thankfully, is nowhere in sight. Giselle thinks he must be on the patio, hovering close to the barbecue. She remembers the party invitations, thrift-store items spelling out PARTY in the black and white chunks of charcoal glowing in a round metal grill.

Giselle approaches Adon. After all, it is his party (or rather, her party for him). "If I eat any more celery stalks, I'll turn into one," he is saying. Whitney laughs too loudly. Giselle tracks down Troy, to make sure he knows that Adon is to have only nonalcoholic beer.

"Sure, dove," Troy responds. "See the promotional bar light? He gets to keep that, too. Don't worry, everything is under mission control. I'm a pro, remember?" He puts his arm around her, gently massaging her upper arm with an oven glove. "I love you," he says.

I don't, Giselle thinks, but knows if she's pushed she'll say, *I love you but I don't* love *you*. Which gives her an idea for Sidonia Burne, who she still hopes to lure away from cats and into a self-help vein.

"Excuse me for a moment, Troy," she says. "You're doing a great job and I have to do one, too." She waves at Sidonia.

Once Giselle has poked into Brad and Sidonia's conversation, she privately offers the cat author the self-help-book suggestion. But Sidonia, like a wet dog in a tile hallway, noisily shakes off the suggestion.

"No, no, no. I'm certain cats are our window to the human world, Giselle. It's by watching them on the window sill, watching the world, that we contemplate what makes our own lives tick."

A commotion at the door draws Giselle, in case an interloper has arrived. But it is Xenia, body-painted like a gypsy in a Lycra jumpsuit. With her is Marni, whom Xenia introduces as the world's leading cat psychic.

"Oh dear," says Giselle under her breath, muffled as if under layers of ermine. Xenia wriggles out of her neon ocelot-spots coat and Marni seductively unzips her leather bomber jacket. "I'll get you all set up in just a moment," Giselle says as she passes the coats to one of Troy's helpers. "But first, how about a drink or some food?"

"Is that where I'll be reading?" asks Xenia as she points to a cabana, a little grass shack in the direction of the barbecue.

Marni smiles. "It's so cold outside a ski chalet might be better—or an igloo." She steps forward to avoid being brushed by a bespectacled young man from *Monotony* who walks hurriedly in accompanied by an editor from sister publication *Dichotomy*.

The latter's editor is a sultry, diminutive skinhead named Sebastiane and she has come to the party to review Glee Club, albeit in speech bubbles over random photos. Her scattershot gaze finally settles on Tammy, making a stir in her side-zipped barnyard jeans, which barely graze the tops of her ankles. Her waist is cinched by a knapsack-cord belt that restrains her sailcloth shirt. The tempestuous musician looks like she's broken free from the mast and is ordering her detractors to walk the plank—over her.

"I'll just introduce myself," says Sebastiane.

"What?" asks Pepper, from the surfing publication and TV show *Off the Lip*. But Sebastiane ignores his query and heads in another direction. Pepper is anxious to meet Adon, aware the teen pop star is to appear in a violent beach-party movie, *Summer Stock*. It's also been rumored his music is about to take a twangy, tubular turn, like surf music played sideways. Pepper spies the backdrop for Troy's performance tonight, a huge photo of the king of surfing, Duke Kahanamoko, propping up his longboard like some rare deep-sea catch, shellacked.

Pepper wraps his arms around himself, both to guard against the cold and accentuate his self-love. He slides the glass door to the right and it comes slightly off its track to wobble at a 15-degree angle. He sees Len keeping a vigil over the barbecue, and initiates introducing himself, offering an afghan-gloved hand.

Len grasps it absently while instructing the a cook to "burn one, take it through the garden, and pin a rose on it." The cook, a boy whose face is equal parts pimples and freckles, ignores him, flipping a lone burger in retort.

"I'll translate for you," Len says to Pepper. "I asked for a burger well-done, with lettuce and tomato and onion."

"I think the condiments are inside, in plastic containers," Pepper replies. "But why did you learn to talk like that?"

"It's interesting you say 'why' and not 'where,' because that is the crux of the matter—the 'why.' Makes me think you're good at asking questions."

"I'm a journalist," Pepper says proudly. "Name's Pepper McCoy."

"I hope you're not a baseball journalist, Pepper, or you'll never get anywhere near the dugout."

"I don't get you."

"*No Pepper* is what the signs say on the fences near the dugout. Didn't you ever notice that?" asks Len.

"Nah. Baseball's an old man's game. Hoop's more my style, hoop and surfing."

Len takes another sip of his frothy, watery draught beer that looks like ocean soup. Thinking of Giselle, he intones "Drinking to remember/ drinking to forget" to a waltz tempo. A hustle of breeze disturbs his reverie as Troy arrives, brought by the chef, fed up with Len's incomprehensible lingo.

"Glad you're back," Len says to the chef. Len is now more than a little drunk and his impaired speech further complicates his orders. "Paint a bow-wow red, gimme shum nervous pudding." The chef leaves, fast.

"Excuse me, sir, my name's Troy."

"That's your misfortune, not mine," Len replies, as clear and forceful as a sunset under Santa Ana conditions.

"My chef tells me you're making his job difficult."

"Maybe he's not much of a chef."

"I can assure you he is," Troy answers. "And if he tells me something or someone is bothering him, then my job is to find out what that is."

Len steps into Troy, pushes him. Troy responds by crossing his elbows, a cigar-store Indian.

"Kaw-Liga, oooh!" sings Len, taking a swing at Troy with his microphone hand.

Adon stands next to Pepper now, and the two follow the scuffle, as if they were spectators at a tournament. Giselle is busy attending to the arrival of Pandra. When Tammy gets word of the row, she rushes to her man's side and lunges for Troy's scrubbed neck.

A booming voice thunders over the PA. "This is Whitney speaking. I'd like you all to get your butts over here to hear my daughter sing. Here she is... where is she? Hey, Culligan Girl!"

Tammy immediately releases her gargoyle grip on Troy and Len drops the paper plate of Jell-O he had poised for Troy's face. "We've got to see this act," she shouts to Len and to the assembled. "We need to know what we're going to upstage."

"Right on!" says Adon.

"Righteous!" agrees Pepper.

Tammy leads the troupe over to the cabana as Adon falls into stride with the wobbling Len. "I'm wondering if you've ever acted," the teen idol asks the inebriated country-and-western star.

"Every day of my life since I lost my girl, kid," Len replies.

"It just that I thought you might like to read for a part in my film, as a heavy. The movie's called *Summer Stock* and Giselle has the details."

"Sure, why not?" Len agrees. "Especially if there's a casting couch."

Casting coach, Adon thinks. *I better find out if we have one of those.* He steps out of the way of a group of revelers headed for Xenia's fortune-telling cabana—and defecting from Frances Culligan's no-holds-barred rendition of "Childproofing."

"It's like Grand Central Station around here," Adon says to Len who suddenly slumps onto the grass, as if he's just lost a game of musical chairs. Seeing Len, Giselle masks her feelings for him, covering them as thickly and completely as a drop cloth over a forged painting.

In truth, the sight of him sends her heart into a Tasmanian tailspin, drowns her in a funnel-shaped chimera cauldron. She's off balance, like a three-wheeled car negotiating a hairpin turn.

After Adon finishes his sampler of songs from *Summer Stock*, Giselle wants to have a word with him. "If you're looking for Adon, he's left with my mom," Frances Culligan pipes up from her perch on a bamboo-backed barstool. "I tried to say good-bye to them, but I couldn't get down."

"Let me get this straight," Giselle says, hoisting Frances to the floor abruptly. "You're telling me Adon left his own party?"

"Uh-huh, with Whitney. Um, gotta go see Glee Club now." Frances darts off with Giselle in pursuit. Outside, Glee Club are wrapping up "Hair Down to Her Butt," a song they describe as their forged-signature tune, it sounds so much like the Runaways' "Cherry Bomb."

As they hightail it off the stage in a flurry, Doris Dismay snarls, "We never do encores." Tammy, however stays behind, frozen in place as though stricken by stage fright.

Tentatively she approaches the microphone, which she shyly taps with her flipping-off finger. "Two-two. Test, test, two," she says and smiles. "I've always wanted to do that."

The leftover crowd, like the now-detached mike, are in

her hands. "I want to introduce you all to someone you may already know. My partner and a helluva lover, Mr. Len Tingle!"

Len storms on stage, tripping and unplugging several leads as he goes.

"It doesn't matter, sweetie," Tammy reassures him. "Our number is unplugged anyway. So if it's broke, we don't need to fix it."

"As long as we ain't broke," Len slurs and strums the introductory chord to "Lucky Stars," now their debut duet. "Tell me I'm crazy; Baby, you're crazy; You're not just being nice?/No I'm not just being nice," they banter in an uneasy key. Len's tension makes the song sound sinister.

When they finish, Tammy bows her head in a gesture of sexual submission. From the audience, Frances Culligan cheers loudest. Giselle puts her thumb and forefinger around the child's tiny wrist and tries to direct her indoors.

"Hey, let go of me!" Frances shouts and adds, as if by rote, "You're not my mother!" She thinks for a moment. "Which is a good thing. Would you like to be my mother?"

Giselle smiles indulgently for the people who are staring. "For heaven's sake, Frances, I'm only thinking of you, of your voice for *Angie Baby*, for your play. This night air is too cold for you to be braying into."

"I wasn't braying," replies Frances, stomping her right foot like a trick horse about to speak or spell. "And if you're taking me anywhere, take me home."

Strood turns up at Giselle's side. "Oh Violet! Do you think you could see that Ms. Culligan here gets home?" Under her breath, Giselle adds, "And that someone's in when she gets there?"

The party is reduced to an inert core group huddled together in the cold. Several look up at a flaming tiki torch as if it were a talisman. Sebastiane from *Dichotomy* lingers deep in conversation with cat-woman Sidonia.

"Wait now, here's Giselle," Sidonia says, taking hold of Giselle's elbow. "Sebastiane here's been trying to talk me into writing a column for her magazine."

"Sounds good," Giselle says, and then thinks it over. "For *Dichotomy*?"

"Yes!"

"It'd be for and about women like Sidonia," Sebastiane explains. "They're independent, self-employed, young at heart if not in calendar years. She's confident, yet concerned. Takes care of business, and of herself."

"And she's thought of a cute little title," Sidonia offers. "She's calling it *The Delicate Eye Area*. It'll be my thoughts and observations, kind of *Diary of a Bad Housewife*–style!" She laughs.

"I love it," says Sebastiane.

Giselle forces a smile, astounded and slightly hurt that Sebastiane, this youngster, has succeeded where she had failed: steering Sidonia away from cat books. Sensing this, Sebastiane winks at Giselle and whispers, "It's all about persuasion."

"I'm thrilled, really," Giselle announces. "I can't wait to read it." She sees Pandra motioning to her, looking as sheepish as someone who turns up at a rock concert wearing a rival band's T-shirt.

"Giselle," Pandra says. "Pandra here wants a word with that fortune-teller of yours." She seems to be unaware she's already met Xenia. "Promise me you'll wait and not shut down the party till I come back out of that hut." She points in the direction of Xenia's cabana.

"Sure," Giselle replies.

As Pandra steps into Xenia's space, Marni emerges, casting a glare of ill-will in the direction of rival cat-expert Sidonia. Briefly, the sun appears and a soft breeze ripples the cabana's bamboo beads as if playing a xylophone.

"What a wonderful whirl!" Giselle exclaims. "It's finally gone tropical—which was supposed to be the theme of this damn soirée."

Violet Strood accompanies Frances home. Frances remonstrates by keeping her tiny hands, which Strood tries intermittently to hold, defiantly close to her chest like a cagey card shark. Their limo driver has informed them his name is Burr. Burr seems ill at ease, his right hand affixed to the windshield-wiper lever as they head into a sudden drizzle.

"I never know what to do in this stuff," he half-growls, half-giggles. "It's not rain, but it's not sleet or snow, either."

Violet resists making any remarks about intrepid mailmen or the Pony Express. And Frances violently pops her gum, like rubber bands ricocheting from braces.

Tired of playing with the windshield wipers, Burr turns his attention to the button that controls the radio. He tunes in K-FROG, an Inland Empire country-music station that must have intensified its broadcast frequency. "A treat for you now," announces the deejay. "The new single from country's hottest rising star, Len Tingle, and his band Highway Hypnosis. Let's hear it for, and let's hear it! 'Give Me the Chance To Say We're Through.'"

"Can we have that back here?" Violet asks the driver, who, after fiddling with various controls, aims the speakers at the rear of the car. The attendant sound is like an empty Nehi pop bottle rolling around in a rumble seat. Len's voice, however, is pure bourbon and crystalline, like warm old radio tubes crossed with skate blades cutting over a frozen moonlit lake.

Violet taps her fishmouth-toed wedged sandal in time, while Frances leans her head onto the seat's armrest. As they draw near her home Strood gently jostles the little girl awake. When she tweaks on her brat pigtails Frances jolts upright like a wooden marionette. "That's my house," Frances fairly shouts. "Those gates, there."

The car stops outside the dark metal fence where a black cat waits, his eyes glowing like Halloween candles. He wears a lavender ribbon around his lower waist, flapper-style. "Spike!" Frances calls. "My mother must have let him out. He was in when we left, I'm sure. My mother must be home."

"Let me take you to the door, anyway," Violet insists.

"No!" says Frances. "That way you'll find out my code, and my mother told me not to let anyone find out the code."

"Well, tell you what. What if I wait here and then you wave to me once you're safe inside."

"Do I have to?"

"I'd like it if you would."

Frances steps down and out of the gunboat limo, refusing Burr's helping hand. At the foot of the gate, she pulls out a river rock the size and shape of a lunch box, climbs atop it and proudly punches in her security code. When she doesn't hear the familiar buzz, she pauses. Frances doesn't want to ask for help, so she rattles the gate. To her surprise it magically glides open. She enters, goes up the walkway and opens the front door with her key on its Barbie keychain. Frances waves good-bye from the doorway, and Violet is driven off into a cold, flimsy, moth-holed blanket of a night.

Frances turns down the hall and heads for the kitchen. She needs two drinks to take to her room: one for now and the other to replenish her bedroom refrigerator, in case she gets thirsty in the night. As her feet hit the kitchen tile, she stops in her tap-dancing tracks: two women are at the dining-room table. She's seen them before, on the way to the bus or to mail a letter. Still, she thinks they shouldn't be here.

"Where's my mom?" Frances asks.

"It's okay," Janine says. "Hermione and I are your baby-sitters. You know, like in *The Babysitters Club*."

"I hate those books. Who are you?"

"My name's Hermione," Hermione says in her safe, Disneyana Hayley Mills voice.

"Would you read me a story?" Frances asks, suppressing a yawn. "After I get Spike?"

Tucked in her canopied bed, under a patchwork quilt where Spike wriggles and growls, Frances drifts off as Hermione reads to her from *Exclusive! The Inside Story of Patricia Hearst and the SLA*.

At a friend's bachelor pad, its walls lined with pictures of the Rat Pack, Whitney holds fast to Adon. Separating requires effort, like undoing a Velcro fastener.

But pull away Adon does. He walks to the bedroom's Cinerama picture window, which looks out onto a cemetery.

"Quiet neighbors," he says, gesturing.

Whitney's grimace adjusts itself to a neutral expression akin to the flat vital sign registered by her husband's body upon arrival at Cedars. She offers Adon champagne, not in a fluted glass but in '60s stemware, blooming in its bowl, the size and shape of her breasts.

"This tickles my nose," Adon says as he sips. Then he appraises Whitney's somber, otherworldly expression.

"I'm thinking about Shaun," she explains. "My husband."

"I know that," Adon replies. "I mean I know who he was—I didn't know you were thinking about him."

"It's been really hard for me to keep going," she says, adjusting a satin slip strap. "My love for him was the greater part of me. I know other people carry on, continue, and even triumph in adversity, through even worse things. But...." She cries, then collects her tears. "I'm just not in their ranks."

Adon sets down his glass. "I wish I could do something to make it better."

"You can't. Well, you could hold me," Whitney says, leaning into his arms.

"What about Frances?"

"Frances!" Whitney seems to scoff. "Frances was born old. She doesn't need me, not at all. She's all Shaun. He rejected me, he rejected her; and she rejected me. She'll be relieved once I'm not around. She'll be like that damn cat, Spike, landing on padded feet."

Adon grasps this, but still he stumbles. "I'm really sorry... sorry Shaun felt he had to die. But I guess... wasn't he really tormented?"

"Tormented, *him*? It's like something I read in a book:

Sometimes, it's the art that creates the suffering in the first place."

"There, there," says Adon, thinking he'll comfort her. "You look like you lost your best friend."

And it's this most inappropriate banality that makes Whitney fall, allows her to will herself into his boyish, guarded arms.

The next morning, at Crazing, Strood thinks she'll be the first one into the office. Then she finds Giselle seated at her desk, wearing a variation on the outfit she wore at Adon's party (created partly from cast-offs from a bag in the office intended for the Salvation Army. She's playing with her collection of matchbooks and has opened several covers to make pyramids. An orange stapler stands in for the Sphinx.

"Hey, hi," Strood says, pleased.

Giselle looks up, her red eyes ringed with tear lines.

"Oh, gosh," says Strood. "Here, let me get you some tea."

"No tea, thanks."

"It's Len?"

"Like hell it is," Giselle replies in a low monotone, as if she's far removed from her feelings.

"Could I tell you the way I see it?" Strood asks.

"Yes, please," replies Giselle. "Especially if it's what I want to hear."

"I think that Len, already really immature, has landed himself a midlife crisis."

Giselle's eyes are now lit like a frozen pond found by sunshine. "He's quit his job," she says softly. "His record is a hit.

He's got everything now."

"Everything, that is, except you."

"Strood, you're an instrument of divine intervention. I just wish that every pop lyric I hear didn't seem personalized and addressed just to me."

"Well," says Strood, as she sits on a window ledge and starts to swing her chunky-heeled shoes, "I've got a theory about that too: All the people who wrote those sad, sad songs, those undying-love ones or those vitriolic and vindictive ones, all the writers—to a man, to a woman—they all got better, or they forgot. I mean, they must have."

"Do you think?" asks Giselle. "I mean I suppose a large percentage of them did. Some music magazine ought to follow up the story." Her phone extension lights up; the office is quiet, and so still they can hear the ringing clearly from down the hallway.

It is Troy calling to tell Giselle how very much he loves her. She winces inside: now that she's more available than ever, she is completely unattainable and, therefore all the more compelling to would-be lovers.

"What are you doing for lunch?" Giselle asks, as if from the floor of a deep pit.

"I was planning to prepare a crisp salad using a new alternative to the cumbersome salad spinner. It's called…"

"I wasn't thinking of food," Giselle interrupts. "How would you feel about driving to the Inland Empire?"

"I do have a growing client base in the Moreno Valley."

"I was thinking more of Corona, of a place on Sixth Street called the Flaming Arrow."

"Barbecue?"

"Motel, Troy."

"Oh," he says and his voice catches and then trails off like the security chain they find strung on the motel's dented plywood door. Their room is spartanly appointed with a TV, a lopsided lamp, and the remote control, all bolted down firmly, as vandal-proof as Giselle wishes to be, on the bed beneath Troy's tanned and fit body.

"I only want to stay here forever," Giselle says, looking away from Troy. "Be part of the furniture."

"I'm sure seeing another side of you."

"Sure I didn't tear you away from your salad spinner?" Giselle turns, with great effort, onto her stomach.

"It can wait. Besides, it wasn't a salad spinner."

Giselle shuts her eyes and tries to block her emotions, and the perception that she's so much like this near-empty L-shaped motel: vacant, almost derelict, and certain to be closed down. Metal shutters will replace the streaked windows already nailed shut; tumbleweeds will fill hedges and block bare-kneed walkways. Neon letter casings will corrode to spell out little ironies that a few aficionados will nudge each other over, with a sigh that bespeaks distance and loss.

Hermione and Janine lie entwined in Whitney's quilt like two taffeta-wrapped holiday crackers. Janine had slept fitfully: the one in possession of logic, she was acutely aware there was no solid reason why Whitney might not return home at any moment. Indeed, as Frances' mother, she should. When the bedside clock-radio alarm kicks in, Janine is already awake, bristling to the disconcerting twang of Len Tingle begging his girlfriend in 4/4 time for the first chance to say it's over between them.

Janine turns her body to twist the dial—the machine is a replica '50s thunderbird-turquoise plastic shoebox—and settles on a duet. "That was Len Tingle with Tammy Whynot," the deejay chirps, "doing a number called 'Lucky Stars,' first recorded by Dean Friedman and Denise Masa all the way back in 1978." The deejay sighs. "'Listen, hon, I know you're dumb/But you don't have to look so glum.' They may not write 'em like that anymore, but I guess we can be grateful they still record 'em."

"Do shut up!" Janine says loudly, conveniently startling Hermione awake in the process.

"Jesus," Hermione says, pulling two copper bobby pins from either side of her deflated hair. "I guess I'd hoped it was all a dream."

"We're in LA, not Dallas or Kansas."

There is a knock at the door, softly twice, before Frances enters her mother's room.

"Shouldn't you check my Day-Runner?" she asks Hermione. "I probably have to be somewhere." She holds out the black, tabbed book, fat as a bound and thumb-indented Bible.

"Sure, sure," Janine says but as she reaches for the book, Frances pulls it away. "I want her to look," she cries, pointing at Hermione. Hermione takes the book and locates the appropriate day, which Frances has denoted with a pink synthetic-fur bookmark in the shape of a worm.

She sees an entry for 2 p.m.: "Rock Star Denny's for keys to Them Park; *Angie Baby* tie-in." The writing slants nearly flat to the left and then rises sharp and round. It belongs to Whitney; Frances' printing, by contrast, is as exacting and labored as an embroidery sampler.

"We need to go out about 1:30," Hermione says. "After lunch."

"Does that mean I can watch cartoons?"

"Sure."

"And you'll lay out what I'm supposed to wear on my bed?"

Hermione hesitates. "Of course," she falters.

Giselle wakes with a smoggy, mid-afternoon headache, the kind that goes with unneeded sleep. She is on the edge of the otherwise empty bed. Troy has made up his half and left a note on a yellow Post-It. *I'm calling on a client,* it says. *Wait for me. I'll be back soon.*

She looks at the phone, the receiver of which is stickered with impossibly detailed instructions—too much tiny type on a narrow strip. Still she stares at it and, like a primitive, wills it to ring and be Len, who'll have found her, have known all along where she is. Instead, its silence hums as loudly as the clumsy air cooler. So she turns on her side to touch herself elaborately, pondering, dumbstruck, how all of a sudden she happened to blunder into the midst of her sexual peak.

Giselle moans, a sound as far from ecstasy as slow-moving despondency can be. It's as if Len's doubts about her were a black spot in the gridlocked traffic of her heart. She knows she must get up, drive back to Hollywood, and return to the day's business. To leave Strood to cope alone is selfish.

Picking up the phone's clumsy receiver, she struggles to decipher the dialing instructions, finally getting an outside line by what seems like default.

Strood answers. "Hiya. I suppose you want to know the lay of the land. Well, low-rolling hills so far. I'm just sitting here with Brad who's brought in some revisions for *Summer Stock*."

"I'll be back in about an hour and a half, tops," Giselle says. And then: "Any word from Len?"

"Not so far. But the record is in there with a bullet. Heavy rotation, picked to click... all the best clichés."

"I've always thought clichés became clichés simply because they were the best."

"Could be. But no, no word."

"If you're talking about Len, he's being written into *Summer Stock*, now that I've taken over," Brad interjects.

"Did you catch that?"

"Yes, can you ask him if he can hang around till I get back? But he shouldn't cancel anything."

From where she's sitting, atop her desk with her long legs draped over Brad's shoulders like suspenders, Strood replies, "Oh I think he'll wait," as she digs her heels into his back.

Whitney emerges from the elaborate bathroom of Adon's borrowed apartment, where she'd showered at length, alone. Adon is on the white naugahyde sofa, arranging himself to avoid its silver-dollar sized buttons. He smiles when he sees her. "I was thinking about sending out a search party."

"Right," she replies dispassionately, flat as a showroom's firm mattress.

"What would you like to do today?" he asks, all sprite

and impish energy—a sugar high. "I ought to phone Crazing, 'cause I think there's something to do with my film... but I can be late."

"Do you think I could move in with you for a while?"

"Babe, you can move in with me forever. Only I guess we should go home first."

"I'll get my things," Whitney says, picking up a minuscule handbag. "Wait, here they are."

It occurs to Adon he might ask about Frances, but he dismisses this, electing to have what there is of Whitney's attention all to himself. He finds the waxy red mouth-shaped phone, lifts its upper lip and speaks into the lower reaches of its cupid's bow. "I'm calling us a car," he tells Whitney, who's looking out over the graveyard. "Come away from that window."

She moves obediently but without conviction.

"Are you hungry?" he asks her. "Because we can get Will to drive us through for some Happy Meals." Hearing this, Whitney almost smiles.

Back at his condo, the clean-up staff is just finishing. Wearing plastic gloves, they load bags of trash into what looks like a van on day-release from the coroner's office. The last item to be packed in is the folded-up fortune-telling hut.

"It was them we were waiting on," one of the cleaners tells Adon. "They were in that hut all night. Shoot." The older man pauses. "All I can say is that dame must have some kind of life ahead of her."

"Or behind her," says his assistant. "You never know with these Hollywood types. Present company excepted of course," he adds, crooking the brim of his baseball cap, the crown of which is embellished with a golfing motif.

Adon turns to look for Whitney; he sees her on the other side of his sliding glass door, curled up on his sofa, watching cartoons.

Frances Culligan rejoices to see her clothes lying rumpled on the bed, as if crudely cut out with snub-nosed scissors for a paper doll. Hermione feels she's done well in her choice of a black poodle skirt, collared sweater, and toy lucite mules with sharp-edged glittering elastic bands across the bridge of the toes. The shoes are placed at the foot of the bed and not on it, as she's aware that shoes on a bed are a warm invitation to bad luck.

"Now we're going to get dressed up, too," Hermione tells her. "Janine thinks we ought to look like the girls in the B-52s."

Janine has gone to collect their car, a gold, sea-oxidized Vega that growls as it runs like some kind of rabid metal windup toy that has spent too many nights on a dew-encrusted lawn. Meanwhile, Hermione bundles Frances out onto the porch, holding her close.

The Vega roars into view, reluctant as the MGM lion, and Frances crinkles her freckled nose which now resembles the gartered elastic on her shoes.

"Am I supposed to go in that?" she demands. "It's like looking at a TV that doesn't have cable."

"It's for fun!" Janine cries from the driver's seat. "It's an ironic statement."

"It still looks like a rustbucket to me," Frances says, climbing into the back seat, littered with waxy, dented Big Gulp cups, their takeaway lids as sharply split as sun-damaged skin.

"Did you know that McDonald's milk shakes never melt?" Frances asks, brightening.

"What do you mean?" says Hermione.

"Just what I said. You can leave 'em in the sun or in the car overnight and they never break down. They always have those fleck things."

"I'll have to try that," Janine replies. "But for now, we're going to Denny's."

"Beats hell out of Disneyland," says the child, kicking the back of Hermione's bucket seat with her open-toed shoes till they arrive. The roof at Denny's, a stark yet bashful building, cries out to be used as a skateboarding ramp.

Seated in a booth and surveying his mosh pit of food is Rodney Bingenheimer, still the unofficial mayor of Sunset Strip. Two booths down, unsheathing a straw for her Tab, is a haunted-looking Pandra. She awaits the arrival of Perry, the mastermind of Them Park, the rock-and-roll theme park this gathering's been called to honor.

A Lego model of the park is behind sliding Perspex doors, next to the gravity-defying pies. A tiny key to these doors, one that would fit a diary, will be presented to young Frances because of her role in *Angie Baby*. In the model, gold stars that traditionally denoted school attendance signify the Rockin' Walk of Fame.

Pandra shifts in her tuck-and-roll vinyl booth, and someone asks if she needs anything. She rapidly blinks her reply, as if to say her vulnerability is their problem, not her own.

A disguised Janine and Hermione usher Frances in, and Rodney goes to greet her where a makeshift stage has been set up alongside the cash register and counter array of cinnamon toothpicks. Introducing Frances, Rodney stands only slightly taller, and the microphone requires little adjustment before Frances breaks into the title song and overture from her upcoming show.

She sings, "You live your life in the songs you hear/on the rock and roll radio," ending with "Angie Baby, you're a special lady/living in a world of make believe/well, maybe."

The diners and the press, including Sidonia, who will write it up for *Delicate Eye Area*, sit spellbound, as if mesmerized by a metronome.

Giselle leaves the Flaming Arrow, but she doesn't have to check out; Troy, after all, will be back. Outside a bar called the Duck Pond she is greeted by a drunken man. "I've seen girls in my time," he says. "But none like you. I mean, there are girls and there are girls... but you, you're a Technicolor Girl!"

As he speaks Giselle reaches down the neckline of her droopy-collared shirt to touch the rhinestone-encrusted cross she always wears for safety and then, while she's at it, tugs her black bra strap. She stops into the corner Circle K store to ask directions back to the freeway: in the sexual disarray she's lost all sense of direction.

Driving back to LA, Giselle is contemptuous of herself for not being able to stop thinking of Len. She scowls as she recalls a friend who told her early on that he wasn't right for her. "You want a man who gets stopped at Customs," the friend advised, "not the kind of man who looks like he'd be conducting the search." Maybe it's true that Len is not exotic or illegal enough for her.

Why then can't she give up on him? Perhaps it's her nature: she can't even give up on a pen as it runs out of ink: she keeps on scrawling sentences, then has to study the blotter or sheet just behind to decipher what she wrote.

And why must she live all aspects of her life as if it were a poetry assignment? It was something Pandra would do, not her.

Giselle switches the radio on, indenting the knob to bring back the staticky, comforting AM frequency. On an oldies station she hears a song that reminds her of Glee Club's "Travel, Meeting People, and World Peace." She feels what she thinks is a shudder, but in truth she's just veered into the left lane, crossing over the raised markers.

Correcting herself, she tries to think about work. "You're supposed to be a professional, for Christ's sake," she scolds, a drill sergeant to her psyche. She gasps when she remembers she's missed Frances' and Pandra's appearances at the Them Park press event. But when she hurriedly calls Strood, the answering machine picks up. "Good girl," Giselle says, high-fiving the rear-view mirror.

"Bad dog," Tammy says to Kachina, out of eye- and earshot of Len who would shudder to find Tammy berating his four-legged love. Kachina had fetched one of Tammy's fun-fur purses and taken it apart. What remains is a plastic skeleton fleshed out with sprouts of Astroturf green. Tammy picks up the stripped-down item and employs it to swat Kachina's hind-quarters, punctuated by her inverted, flagging comma of a tail.

The dog retreats while Tammy goes to the fridge for some orange juice. Kachina watches from a bend in the breakfast bar, thinking perhaps she'll be fed or have her water dish replenished from the built-in spout.

Instead, Tammy pours a glass of juice for herself and a tumbler-sized one for Len, who is sleeping off a tiger-patterned hangover. She walks past Kachina to the bedroom, where she bangs Len's glass down on the bedside table his spinning head is turned toward. When Len fails to stir, she goes into the starburst-motif bathroom and starts to fill the tub. Sitting on the narrow ledge, she watches the water creep up.

On a soap-caked wicker shelf, Len's reading glasses (his tribute to Buddy Holly) serve as paperweight to his unbound *Summer Stock* script. Tammy picks up the sheets and reads them. She seethes just as the paper does as it buckles in the steam. There must be a part for her in here somewhere.

Sliding into water so hot it feels like sun-baked black sand, Tammy remembers when she told Glee Club boss Hedda Hop-head that she was fucking Len.

"Him?" her honcho had queried, astonished. "Why, he's only borderline fuckable, at best."

"As opposed to what?"

"Free-verse fuckable. No margins, no meter."

"You mean like when you always come," Tammy said, not asked.

"Come? Coming's a confidence trick, like throwing your voice."

Plugging the tap with her unadorned big toe, Tammy makes a spray from a cascade of cold water. That last remark was where she'd lost the plot with Hedda—that idea that sex combines a con game with ventriloquism. So far have she and the group's manager fallen out that Tammy fears dully for her place in Glee Club. The duet she'd recorded with Len was, to Hedda, "low church and high treason," and Hedda had warned her to put more into Glee Club or "go back to your truckstop portable."

Yet Tammy knows she's getting the last laugh. "Lucky Stars" is selling well, and she has her own plans to cut an answer record to Len's "Give Me the Chance To Say We're Through" with a session musician from South Dakota she'd once given a 7-Up and No-Doz blow job.

In the midst of her reminiscence, the bathroom door opens and her white robe hanging on a hook heralds Len's appearance like a choral ghost.

"Hi," she greets and he winks at her from his stance over the toilet bowl. When he joins her in the tub, the water is displaced to the upper reaches of her broad shoulders. She fingers her crotch and leans toward Len's left ear.

"Come on in," she says, beckoning with her hand. "The water's fine."

Entering her, Len obliges. Once he's come she leans back, resting one foot on the tub's spout. "In your movie," she begins.

"I don't think it's my movie, sweet."

"You know what I mean." She scoops what remains of the dwindling bubbles and makes a bra for her boyish chest. "In *Summer Stock*..."

"Stock as in soup."

"What?"

"Nothing," Len replies, missing Giselle.

"Do you think there's a part for me in the movie?"

"A screwball siren?"

"A who?"

"I can ask, honey. But remember it's not my movie. I don't call the shots."

"Not even sound effects or something?"

"Somehow I can't picture you in a corner, clapping two coconut shells together," he says, his palms covering her pearl-beaded breasts.

By the time Violet Strood and Brad arrive at Denny's, the crowd has dispersed and the PA is dismantled. Only Sidonia remains, scrawling hieroglyphic shorthand into a flecked spiral notebook. Violet reminds Sidonia who she is: "Giselle's tattooed right hand, the one that says H-E-L-P."

"Oh, hi," says Sidonia, barely glancing up through her diamanté-trimmed half-glasses.

"What did we miss? This is Brad, by the way."

"I don't like to paraphrase my notes." Sidonia turns away, her left arm creating a hillside for the valley she's written.

"I'm glad I didn't sit next to her in Junior High," Violet whispers to Brad. "Should we leave?"

"I don't know," he replies, studying an iced tea. "I could always drop by and see how the set construction is going."

"I thought everything took place at the beach. You know, a few beach towels, sand, a Frisbee or two..."

"The exteriors, yeah. But there's also the Surface Club, the bathrooms, changing stalls, outdoor showers."

"I hate those."

"Oh, but they're great for the violence. They really go together. Then there's the Conch Shell Amphitheater...."

Giselle is surprised to find the office locked: Strood should have returned by now. She puts down her bag and settles into her desk chair, startled by an impromptu gulp from the glass water cooler. At an odd angle to a tidy pile of letters, jutting out like a card to be picked, is one stickered *Recorded Delivery*, which must have been signed for by Strood. Giselle opens it, using a plastic knife from El Pollo Loco.

Watermarked bond paper and raised letterhead stress the gravity of the sender and the message: Len Tingle, it transpires, is being sued for copyright infringement by one Carole Mare, a comedy country singer who claims she wrote "Give Me the Chance To Say We're Through," which she'd titled "Button Your Lip with SuperGlue." Mare, a former porn star known for a film called *Secretary Spread* (tag line: "I'll just see if he's in"), is currently making headway as an X-rated Minnie Pearl.

Giselle knows she must phone Len—even though he presumably already knows about it: why should she be the only one to receive the letter?—but makes her first call to Crazing's attorney instead, leaving a plaintive message. After she hangs up, she looks out her window. The sun breaks through, and the sudden glow feels like a mistake.

The afternoon drags with neither a call from the attorney nor the return of Strood. Giselle goes home to her still apartment—not even the dust stirs—and vehemently kicks off her unconsoling shoes. She thinks back on the day: the motel with Troy, the non-carpool lane-crawl back, underscoring their solitary sex, the absence of Strood, the lawsuit. Yes, the lawsuit.

And then it sinks in. Len was probably seeing Carole Mare during the time Giselle was still with him. And it's this anti-epiphany that causes her, still wearing her work clothes, to cry. She throws off what dime-store and souvenir-shop jewelry she wears—minute copper rattlesnake earrings she'll need a metal detector to retrieve, a rhinestone brooch held to its clasp with paste, a three-tiered simulated-pearl bracelet that tailspins like a twister.

She tears at the collar of her antique blouse and it comes away like tissue paper enfolding an intimate gift. She learns then that falling apart is not an exact science: there's no finite end.

Scolding herself for being out of control, Giselle feels valueless. No price tag, no sale. She manages to get up, and snags the heel of her tights on a wood shard of floor not covered by ragtag carpet. At her sideboard she retrieves a metal candy tin of mementos and searches for a letter from a guy she'd broken up with years ago—someone she knew around the time she first met Pandra.

She finds the card and slips it from the acid-free envelope to read: *Giselle. Going out with you was like heroin. I'm taking up smoking, hoping there's something harder to kick.* As she puts the card down, she feels uplifted—then thinks better of it. *Yeah, right*, she says to herself. *So dating me was a brief rush followed by nodding out, topped off by being sick.*

"The lifeguard stand I see as a metaphor, a lookout/lighthouse reassuring in its triumphant, solidly built safety...." In Brad's single apartment, in the humid, tangled crotch of Mount

Hollywood, he is still providing a scene-by-scene for Strood, unaware that she's fallen asleep astride him.

Morning strains to arrive for Giselle. For Len, Adon, and Brad it means an early call to be on the beach for *Summer Stock*. Len has stayed up most of the night, fronting to his closet mirror and fleshing out the tough-guy persona of his character, Ciro Mocambo. Tammy had left after dinner, applying an extra coat of Maybelline Moisture Whip lipstick, masking her distaste for the food and for him.

Giselle is transfixed by the lore of the dog days, as if these burnt ends of summer offer two compelling possibilities: what is broken remains forever in sharp pieces; what is repaired will no more fall asunder. She applies the superstition to her love life first, then to her work as if by proxy.

"I'm losing my edge," she whispers to her dusty reflection in the pond-colored TV screen she watches by rote as she eats a bowl of Cheerios. Retrieving her image, it's as if she's picking herself up after the previous night's sleepy meanderings. But lately her nocturnal life seems superimposed on her workaday self, the two becoming as sticky and inseparable as two opposing pieces of Saran Wrap, about which Troy no doubt would have something to say.

Thumbing through her cumbersome diary much the way her mother used to read the Bible with the assistance of a pamphlet called *The Upper Room*, Giselle surveys the day's schedule as dispassionately as an auditor.

- *Summer Stock* goes to beach location
- Frances Culligan: premiere of *Angie Baby*

- Pandra: film rights for *Charm School*
- Perry: Them Park opening

It's a red letter day, she surmises. Now, which one will be the red herring? With a twinge she remembers a piece of whimsy from the fledgling days of her business, back when it was Stage Diving, not Crazing. She would thumb through the pages of her spiral-bound desk diary and see the empty days, filled in with nothing more than New Moon, First Quarter, Full Moon, and the occasional holiday. "Let me check my schedule," she would jest. "No, the only thing I have then is Last Quarter."

Adon wakes up next to Whitney, who is as disheveled as an overstuffed chest of drawers. He is quick to embrace her and then descend horizontally—a dolly on a track—to give her oral sex. When he feels she's satisfied, by the way she curls her muscles like a fireside cat, he leaves the bed for the bathroom and gets ready for the beach, for the first day of *Summer Stock*'s location work.

"Is that the time?" he yelps from the shower where he twists the soap on a rope–style waterproof radio. Whitney doesn't answer; she's turned on her side and lost to sleep. When she wakes, it isn't as Adon leaves, but rather when he returns to pick up a copy of the script. "I'd forget my head if it wasn't screwed on," he tells her.

"I wouldn't," Whitney smiles, gesturing through the sheets toward her sex.

He kisses her forehead and then leaves for the day's work. Arriving at the crowded shore, scattered with props like a sandbox, he apologizes to the director: "I'd be late for my own funeral."

"In a way it is," the woman replies. "You might say it's the death of Adon and the birth of Don Loper." She's referring to his onscreen persona. By now Len, biting into an elephant ear that sends crystals of sugar scattering like cartoon sand and asterisks, is already in his tuxedo, eager to impersonate Ciro Mocambo, beach-club proprietor.

Adon approaches him, using his outstretched hand to signify an emphatic hello. Then the younger man turns his attention to the folding table filled with catered food. He picks up four finger-shaped biscuits.

"What is this stuff?" Adon asks, taxing his dental work as he crunches heartily.

"Biscotti," replies a man from Glad, the craft service.

"Biscotti," he repeats thoughtfully. "Hey, it's good, great even. The greatest thing since sliced bread." He laughs at his presumed bon mot, a guffaw catalogued by Sidonia, who's doing a piece on entertainment-crew food, to be titled "Graze Anatomy." Her *Delicate Eye Area* column for *Dichotomy* has been enough of a success that she's now writing a major portion of the magazine. Her stories and tips are already cultish— particularly the one on how to make semi-sheer potholders out of old negligees.

The work has given her a reason to be, to breathe, and its multifarious facets allow her to vent a variegated personality, blowing both dust and air as though from a cube-shaped cooler atop a desert shack. It's as if she's got several pairs of secondhand shoes that all nearly fit. As for her present assignment, Sidonia is barely familiar with Adon's career: she knows him to be a pretty pop star of minimal gifts.

So for the moment she finds herself on a sandlot beach, taking in the action while remaining aloof, a prodigal daughter at a family reunion. Her writing shows that she feels for her characters; yet what is unique is her capacity for distance, a kind of Red Rover game that involves a swapping of places while retaining the original perspective.

Summer Stock's first beach scene unfolds rather than enfolds. Adon as Don Loper tangles with tough guy Ciro Mocambo in a cloying, slimy manner that puts Sidonia in mind of shallow-water seaweed worrying at her ankles. It is more nuisance than menace. She glances at her grotesque Disneyana watch and anticipates her next move. At 11 a.m. she is due at a press conference for the opening of the play *Angie Baby*, starring Frances Culligan, the child star she's been covering in counterpoint to the Adon piece. There she can compare a juvenile repast with the present, pubescent one.

Sidonia bites into an apple fritter tentatively, as if she anticipates having to retrieve a rodent hair from her incisors.

In a tiny recording studio in Echo Park, Tammy approaches the microphone with an Eskimo kiss, kittenish. Her nose scratches the wire mesh, making a washboard sound which causes Zeb, her Dakota musician friend, to recoil as if he's heard plastic nail extensions scratching a baize-green board.

One vehement take finds Tammy completing her calculated answer song to Len's "Where Were You When I Was Falling in Love?" Her timing is apt on another score, too: Glee Club is bringing out its LP, *Agog*, in the klieg-like absence of Tammy.

Tammy's song, "With Your Band While You're Too Slow To Wonder," ought to be the perfect foil—a triptych visor resting on the vulnerable neck of a sun-worshiper.

A game of Ultimate Frisbee is going awry, looking more like a gray and spiked bout of Rollerball in the overcast, heavily polluted midday. The Summer Stalker, Adon's chief rival, moves to even the score with the archer's equivalent of a body blow.

Len Tingle stands alone; not in character but not himself either. He casts a look at a man wearing a waxy, badly screened Hawaiian shirt and, in response, the man moves closer. Something tells Len to be spooked, to be driven into the sea, and he breaks for it. The man in the shirt gives chase as action on the film shifts over to life.

Sidonia clenches her pen in disbelief. Len runs fully clothed into the ocean pursued by a man waving a roll of paper over his head, as if to spank a bad dog. Len tumbles with a wave, but not before being served with a summons from Carole Mare, the paper clinging to his chest like a soggy permission slip.

Later, Len dries off in the sun and the glow of more publicity. He remembers Carole, all right. As George Jones once put it, "her neckline was low, but my spirits were lower." That he stole her song is unlikely: no doubt it is a metaphor for other thefts: that of her trust, her heart, her hopes. He recollects how he'd assured her—a staggering promise as he was lit up at the time and couldn't have written a line any more than he could have walked one—that he'd gently guide her career out of its jagged, jokey terrain and into the lush and deep valley of serious, pure country.

Their affair had taken place during one of his many departures from Giselle, at a time when he'd found it easier to actualize how much he missed her by being with someone else. That Carole will now cost him dearly, he knows. Tammy will be none too pleased and for Giselle it will be beyond the pale. And it's Giselle he longs for—to hear her voice when he apologizes, when he reverently flicks tears from her cheeks with his fingers.

But to call Giselle now would appear a use and a ruse, Len thinks, remembering a fight in which she called him "a user *and* a loser, which tells us how good you were at the first thing." No, his course of action must be instead the only thing he knows: the path of least resistance. In other words, he'll round up the band the way he did those shopping carts, and go out on the road.

His album, *99 and 44/100% Pure Heartache*, is slated for release next month. Sales of both singles are healthy, and his label is pressing him to tour in support of it. Hell, they'd probably be happy to arrange some additional dates. As for *Summer Stock*, well, acting isn't really for country stars, anyway—just look at poor Elvis.

With the prospect of escape, Len's soul vaporizes into release. He unceremoniously walks off the beach set and drives to a Mexican diner, where he quickly orders "Guess Water."

"¿Como?" asks the pockmarked young man working the counter.

"Give me a bowl of your best menudo."

The boy nods in comprehension. "Hangover?"

"Hanging by a thread, but hanging on." Len knows the thread is the unbroken line of the open road.

As filming of *Summer Stock* breaks up for the day, the director is miffed that his best action was both unscripted and irrelevant. And where was Brad, the screenwriter? Had he turned into William Faulkner or Scott Fitzgerald already? What did he think this was, *The Day of the Locust*? Give someone a bungalow...

Giselle arrives on the dumbstruck set. She heads for Adon's trailer, where he clues her in.

"So he's been served?" she verifies.

"Yeah, as sure as the LAPD."

Giselle has a perplexed look. "What?"

"You know. *To Protect and To Serve*. What it says on the side of cop-car doors. Always makes me want to ask for a double cheeseburger and a malt."

Giselle is stunned that Adon could offer any observation other than the most well-trodden cliché. "Well," she says, aware she must turn her thoughts to him, "how are you, anyway? How did it go today?"

"Great, apart from Len. But, you know, even that was cool."

"Was anyone else around?" she manages.

"That chick from *Dichotomy* magazine. Maybe some TV, I don't know."

"Anyone still around?"

"Nah. They all kind of left as soon as Len dried off."

Compared with the events at *Summer Stock*, the press conference for *Angie Baby* is unpromising, Sidonia thinks, settled in her mangy velveteen chair in the converted movie palace.

So jaded is she that she fails to remark the nonappearance of Frances Culligan. As it happens, Frances' absence is overshadowed by the arrival of the resurrected Rory Otis, who's ushered in by Rodney Bingenheimer. But Sidonia shrugs that off, too, having no idea who the former star is, or what the fuss could possibly be about.

Meanwhile, Frances is being hidden and held for ransom by Janine and Hermione, since Janine feels, mistakenly, that mother Whitney is closing in. "I keep seeing her," she tells Hermione. "Like a hippie singer, all dressed in layers and flapping a wet baby blanket."

"Sounds like surrender," Hermione attempts.

"Not likely. This woman's a harridan. She wants to use that wet towel to slap us, like a bully in PE." And so the two women abscond with their charge, returning her not to the flatland confines and comfort of her Hollywood home but to a mountain hideaway with a cactus connection. Frances goes willingly with her adult playmates. "I'd *have* a mommy again," she confesses to Hermione. "But only if she were this tall." She pinches her thumb into her forefinger, as if measuring out grains of salt.

Again Giselle arrives too late to see almost everyone, including Sidonia; she's frustrated at missing the event, though pleased not to run into Whitney, her least-favorite person next to Pandra. The press conference had broken up early, she will later discover, partly on account of Frances Culligan's no-show, but also because Rory invited everyone on hand to his "party in a boxcar" at Union Station. The few people who remained were outside Rory's sphere of influence and never went downtown.

Giselle phones Strood from a gilded box in the old theater, which makes her think of the scene in *The Blob* where the monster invades the cinema and provides the audience on-screen and off with another layer of thrill. As she waits for Strood to answer, she remembers how she once tried to convince Len that *The Blob* was really a metaphor for menstruation and men's fear of it.

In response he'd playfully cuffed her ear and told her to try not to think about things so much. She'd felt relief.

Curiously, there is no answer at Crazing—and no messages to retrieve. Giselle is in the dark. But at her home, which feels as airless as a Grant Wood painting, the light on her answering machine blinks slowly, a laconic wink she recalls would often signal an after-hours communication from Len. Giselle's thought is on target: as she presses *play* she hears Len's slow tones.

"I just need a break," he says. "A break from my life, and from that movie. From that, I need more like a divorce. I want the road, and shows, and you...." He pauses. "I mean, I knew you'd understand."

As ever, it's not her he needs—it's her understanding. Giselle plops her backpack down onto a dining-room chair, and tries not to sigh. Her situation with Len is a useless attempt at closure, about as plausible as folding a thousand-page tome into a perfumed envelope.

Before she finally falls asleep that night, she hums the torch song "What'll I Do?" to her spool-like trouble dolls, lately her preferred method of prayer. When she gets to the lyric "What'll I do with just a photograph/to tell my troubles to?"

she stalls, for now she knows there's no one to listen. Her life feels like it's conducted with a rod just above her head, a sort of surge protector where a magic wand might have been.

The next morning, to Giselle's surprise, Strood is in the office when she gets there.

"What's this about Len being on tour?" Strood asks, with uncharacteristic abruptness.

"It's all true. The *99 44/100% Pure* Show is on the road," Giselle replies. "He's even hooked up with that trailer-park band, Stucco."

"Stucco? But they're not country!"

"He's crossing over. I'm sure there's room for a joke about a chicken there somewhere."

"Well," says Strood. "I have some news. I'm pregnant."

Giselle just stares as Strood continues. "It's Brad's, Brad's and mine, of course. The trouble is, all my friends hate him, and all his friends hate me. It's as if no one in the world likes us together but...." Here she sobs isolated and elegant jewel-like tears. "When we're alone, you see, he's so very, very kind."

"Hey, there," Giselle says softly. "If it's worth anything, I'm happy for you."

"Oh, thank you. I know things aren't rosy for you. I mean, I know you have Troy, though, but..."

"This isn't about me. That you're happy gives me hope, something I've been lacking of late. I mean, you *are* happy, right?"

"I think so. I just keep getting chills, which my mother

always told me is a harbinger of bad luck."

"I'd say don't let hand-me-down superstitions stand in for mixed emotions. Of course, I'm a fine one to talk. But there I go, trying to make this about me."

"I'm sorry, too, I mean I know I've been no good here at the office. I didn't make it to either of yesterday's events, *Summer Stock* or the thing with Frances Culligan."

"I almost did," says Giselle. "But I was late."

"That's my line. I mean, that's how I broke the news to Brad. I said 'I'm late' over and over. It got to where I sounded like the White Rabbit. Oh!" she collapses into giggles. "Rabbits! Do you think there's some significance?"

"You must have quite a mother," Giselle replies. The phone rings in two octave tones. She answers, then listens, nodding faintly. After the call, she asks Strood, "When did you last see Frances Culligan?"

"I-I'm not sure."

"It seems she didn't show up for the press conference yesterday. Not only that, but Rory—you know, the body in Pandra's memoir—just rose from the dead and stole all the headlines."

"What should we do?" Strood asks.

"I'm just running through in my mind who might know what's going on." She calls Whitney Culligan but gets no answer. And Pandra's phone is off the hook.

"I know!" she says then, snapping her fingers. She picks up the phone, thumbs through her Rolodex like a hot dog shooting Waimea Bay. "Sidonia? Hi, it's Giselle."

"Oh, hi," Sidonia responds, listless as an inept doorperson.

"I was wondering if you saw Frances Culligan yesterday.

What went on at the press conference?"

"Who? What? Oh yeah, well... I stopped by for a while, but there didn't seem to be much of a story. That is, after the scene at *Summer Stock*. It was all pretty anticlimactic after that. Some older guy, Rory something, showed up, and that caused a bit of a stir, I don't know why. Adon might have some idea about Frances. He's said to be seeing Whitney."

"He is? Okay, I'll call him. Thanks." Giselle hangs up with her index finger, then taps in Adon's number. But she fails to make a connection. The day drags into afternoon, and she still has no leads on either—any—of her clients. By the time Troy phones, the early evening feels just as disjointed as the preceding hours; she arranges to go to his stationary trailer (his second home) for the night, for the illusion of permanence.

In his box-framed bed they watch an old movie. Bad reception causes it to crackle with a column of snow, an isolated pillar suggesting both time travel and birdcaged go-go dancers. Rabbit ears, even at impossible angles, are no help. Giselle tries to camouflage the devout depression she feels, the sense that each bottom to her life has given way to a lower one.

Troy says, "Len was crazy to get rid of you."

"Yeah, well." Giselle strains with the realization that she must soar above Len and his world like a crop-duster. If he doesn't love her, he isn't who she thought he was. For the moment, this train of thought works like a line of elephants progressing trunk to tail.

Now Troy starts his campaign, toying with Giselle in hopes that if he comes up short, she will long for him.

"I've just remembered I have to go out for a while," he says as he retracts his arm from its perch on her shoulders and neck. Giselle feels mildly challenged, which translates to her heart as an insult, but she says nothing: after all, her evening's TV viewing is fully booked, so how bad could she feel? She does however make a mental note that Troy doesn't kiss her before disappearing out the aluminum-framed door.

She shapes his thermal blanket to hug every contour of her body and provide the illusion that she is loved. Then she settles in to watch *Dillinger*, which she knows will allow her to think of Len, to wallow in her memory of him, uninterrupted for about two hours. That the film is on tonight, while her love for him is in ascendance, is another example of how much she is dogged by synchronicity.

In the middle of the movie, she picks up one of Troy's Tupperware press releases and begins to compose, on the back of it, a personal ad.

Nondescript woman, brown hair, brown eyes, shallow as she is deep, needs cat, seeks man as passionate as he is dispassionate, full-faced, heart-wrenching twang, frequent absences, must have guitar. She draws a line through everything that comes after *seeks* and writes above it, the greater part of the equation, *Len Tingle*.

"I'll be looking at the moon," she recites to the screen, to him, "but I'll be seeing you."

Out on the road, Frances Culligan plays travel games with Hermione in Janine's new used powder-blue Maverick. At home with Len, the dog Kachina seems to grow smaller as she watches Len prepare to leave.

"You're too little for the hangdog routine," Len tells her,

but the dog keeps overacting.

"Any more soap-opera stuff and I'll think you want a bath," Len taunts. Kachina, understanding the closing phrase, shakes energetically in happy anticipation of his touch.

A car with a vanity plate overtakes the Maverick and Hermione muses on its cryptic message: "*Set Dresser*. Let's see. *Set Dresser meets Y B Poor in...*" A truck in the left lane provides a smorgasbord of out-of-state options. "*Idaho.*"

Frances giggles with delight at the story in motion, unfolding just for her. Janine, at the wheel, is busy formulating the ransom note she'll send from their motel halfway up the Donner Pass.

Now that Tammy is officially out of Glee Club and her answer-song has some kind of legs, even if only in a nose-thumbing sense (she pictures the contortions), her former band is combusting from within like the dud log cabin in a five-dollar box of old fireworks. Glee Club's recent effort *Outskirts* featured a raucous cover of "Johnny Get Angry," but it still got lost in a jukebox shuffle of platters.

There is only room for one song this season, it seems, and that song belongs to Len Tingle. Recorded live on the 99 44/100% Tour and released in the midst of the publicity surrounding Carole Mare's charges—which the scandal sheets have dubbed the Birthday Suit—Len's single, "Everything I Own Is in the Back Yard, Everything I Owe Is Inside," has become a huge hit.

The back yard in the song is a kidney-bean shaped plot of threadbare grass pounded and patrolled by a mixed-breed, mangy hound chained to a metal stake like a tether ball.

One day the dog, Porter, digs a hole under the chicken-wire fence. Rescued by a cowgirl in a green pickup truck, he is taken to a new life on a wide-open big-sky ranch. Thus the narrator comes to see what freedom looks like: "His back yard's the back forty/mine's back taxes/Porter got the girl/I got the glasses," he laments. The song is heard everywhere and with such frequency it becomes a vast and melancholy collective memory, a little like "Happy Birthday."

The song does it all for Len, who is now so famous that when he orders "blowout patches and hen fruit" no one has to question that what he's trying to camouflage is an order of pancakes and eggs.

The lawsuit with Carole Mare is soon settled out of court—but not before she gathers heaps of publicity for her country-porn business enterprise, Corn Pone. Its impact on Tammy is even farther-reaching, and she reacts the only way she can—by taking out her hurt on Kachina, who comes to physically embody Tammy's feelings of being left out, of being hungry, of being in the way.

But while Tammy is agonizing and Kachina suffering, what's taking place is a kind of shell game. Len has replaced all of them—Tammy, Giselle, Carole—with a girl he met on tour. Mabel works the T-shirt concession. He fell for her one night when she came to his tour trailer, clad only in a University of Wisconsin nightshirt with her blond hair bunched and braided like a candlestick, a sleepwalker's nightlight.

Mabel had arrived seeking a nightcap and they ended up in bed, Len hovering over her, holding her close to him and under him. He wanted to break into song, to burst into a rousing chorus of "On Wisconsin" like the bearcat he momentarily believed himself to be.

Because Len feels the affair with Mabel must be kept secret from the crew and the band, he devises a method of letting her know when he can see her: he'll either perform or have played on the PA the song "Just Walk On By/Wait on the Corner." Mabel is thus hampered: she can neither say no nor convey exactly when she might want to see him.

A member of the road crew, doubling as intrepid tabloid informer, breaks the story to her paper, who gives it front-page treatment under the banner *T-SHIRTS AND SYMPATHY*.

When Tammy reads this, she swiftly writes a song for her new band, "My Lover Went on the Road (And All He Brought Me Was This Lousy T-Shirt Girl)," and moves out of Len's apartment, leaving Kachina behind. A couple of days later, she places telephone calls to the SPCA and the scandal sheets. The latter relish the tie-in of a singer-songwriter who profits from the story of a dog and yet abandons his own. The paper uses a mock-up of the lasso "L" in Len's logo to encircle Kachina gallows-style. In a game of hangman, Len Tingle has been second-guessed.

The story comes to light as Len is holding a press conference to acknowledge his involvement with Mabel, who has not joined him. "Yeah, I miss her to the hilt," he jokes, "or at least to the Hilton." Yet with at least one questioner his joke falls flat. The journalist stands, asks Len about his abandonment of Kachina, and stuns the performer into silence. It's as if a dank speech bubble hangs over his head like a jellyfish.

Sidonia is not at the press conference, having been demoted by *Dichotomy* for missing both the disappearance of Frances Culligan and the resurrection of Rory Otis. About the time Frances and Hermione, passengers still, have resorted to using bumper stickers for their road stories' dialogue (Hermione: "PS I Love You"; Frances: "Go Climb a Rock"), Sidonia is trying to come to terms with her new assignment, a travel column she hopes to call *Other People, Hell*. At her computer she works on her introductory lines: "Jean-Paul Sartre may have been on to something when he wrote that other places are heaven and other people, hell. The problem is, there is no place I want to go."

She looks at her '60s-style floral-fabric suitcase. She must fill it, like this screen, for her first assignment, a golf-cart parade in a retirement community near Palm Springs. "Hi-Balls in the Lo-Desert" she titles it, before setting foot out the door.

Alone in the office, dwarfed by a seven-story mountain of messages, press clips, pleas, faxes, calls, deadlines, and police activity—the seven deadly sins, thinks Giselle, realizing her sequential thoughts involve two sevens and constitute a match, like snake eyes. She sits immobilized—thinking not of where Frances might be, what to do about Len, when to respond to an urgent call from Pandra—but about dice and whether they actually have sevens on their faces. Or do you roll a four and a three, a five and a two, a six and a one to reach the lucky number? Where could she find a pair of dice? Even fuzzy dashboard ones would do.

Giselle knows Strood would have the solution, but Strood has long since sidestepped her sidekick role, to the point where Giselle knows she should fire her.

In fact Strood and Brad are but a short distance away, driving along the loopy road that runs through Forest Lawn Cemetery, Glendale, from which Brad draws occasional inspiration. He particularly likes the pristine road signs, which are both vintage and unvandalized.

Strood is not impressed and remarks only that there are a lot of empty parking spaces. "I don't think old Forest Lawn is holding its own as a tourist attraction," she remarks. "Maybe it needs some thrill-spilling rides, a blast through the crematorium or something."

Brad doesn't respond but steers her inside and towards a huge stained-glass window depicting the Last Supper, which is theatrically unveiled each half-hour, rain or shine, accompanied by piped-in narration. He chooses chairs in front of a statuary grouping called Day and Night. "Salt and Pepper," Strood renames the male and female figures. The message begins to play, announcing that the panel depicting Judas broke five times. "Oh, my word," Strood gasps, "they're going to recreate the picture minus Judas! I just know it!"

"Shhh," says Brad. At the conclusion of the program, he pulls her right up close to the window. Casement lead crisscrosses the folds in the Last Supper tablecloth.

"Marry me," Brad says. "I had to take this window of opportunity to ask you."

"I hate that phrase," Strood protests. "It makes me want to defenestrate."

"But I accept," she continues, realizing all is not lost: carved on a nearby crypt, she's found a name for her baby: Cleve.

Frances sleeps through a large chunk of the Central Valley, that most utilitarian landscape of dishwater-mopped linoleum. Janine is still formulating the ransom note she will write, having abandoned the idea of culling pages from a Brat Pack novel. An earlier time now captivates her, and a kidnapping she'd recalled when she first hatched her plan—that of the Lindbergh baby.

She plans to suggest Death Valley's Zabriskie Point as a drop-off point, but it will be a red herring, a bum steer. Instead, a High Sierra town called Black Mesa is her destination, where they'll hole up like knotty pine. The clapboard house she's rented has layers of weather-beaten black and white shingles, resembling an overworked clapperboard. "Scene Four, Take 15. Frances is tied to the railroad tracks." Janine laughs, alone.

Giselle drives to Hawaiian Gardens where she goes to a bar called the Castaway to ask if they have any dice. They don't, the bartender drones, but the Horseshoe Club in Gardena ought to be able to oblige her. Giselle has two lo-balls, then worries about the time. Frantically scanning the peeling bamboo walls for a clock, she finds what she thinks is one, only it turns out to be a thermometer.

Avoidance, she thinks, my Achilles heel. It has never been more imperative in her career at Crazing for her to be responsible, yet she sits in a bar, debilitated by the thought of Len.

Resolving to forget about the dice (which never cared about *her* anyway), Giselle steps out into the harsh yet indirect light, which refracts off the platinum and chipped-concrete curb. She puts on her cat's-eye sunglasses and elects to walk several blocks to buy overpackaged bottled water from a bare-bones liquor store. As she drives back to the office, she decides her first order of business must be not Len, not Frances, but Pandra.

Pandra lies on the earth-toned padded bedspread in her Travelodge room, contemplating the telephone conversation she's just had with Perry, who again pressed her to attend the grand opening of Them Park. Since Frances Culligan is now unconfirmed, Perry has asked Rory to throw the switch that will electrify a skyscraper-size Fender Stratocaster. And Rory wants Pandra to be there too.

She folds the *National Intruder,* dominated by stories about Rory and Frances. Whitney has been quoted saying she's neither worried about nor affected by her daughter's absence: "Frances will land on her feet, not her buttered side." The item bumps Len Tingle and his impounded dog off the Impulse page of the tabloid.

Pandra calls Reese, who has elected to stay on in Mexico, but she can't get through to him. Rory, however, returns her call.

A new arrival at the SPCA has generated nearly as much attention as Len Tingle's Kachina. Spike, Frances Culligan's black cat, had been cared for by neighbors who, on hearing of Kachina's plight, thought another lesson should be taught, and turned the animal in.

With Len away and awash with his new love (and screenwriter Brad ditto), Adon has lost interest in *Summer Stock.* Shooting is suspended, which affords him time to lavish on Whitney, still eerily unperturbed about her absent daughter.

Adon tells Whitney he's refusing to return to the set of his film. "If I go there any more, they'll have to start charging me rent," he explains. The upshot is that in the coming months he'll enter into what are essentially his Wilderness Years.

FROM ADON TO ANON muses a formerly fawning teen magazine. "Adon's been in the wilderness so long," a columnist remarks, "he might as well set up his own dude ranch."

"Nonsense," he retorts in a letter to the editor. "I've got lots of irons in the fire."

From her perch overlooking the giant guitar, Giselle observes Pandra and Rory, each with a rather tentative arm around impresario Perry, as they turn on the switch that unleashes a G-A-C chord progression.

When Strood had asked her what Rory's return would mean for Pandra's book, Giselle replied, "It could go either way, become an exercise in futility or fortuity."

"It looks like they might be getting together."

"In that case, an exercise in late-breaking fertility?"

Further surveying the crowd, Giselle spies Len. He resembles not her beloved man-in-the-moon of yore, but an overblown Thanksgiving Parade balloon.

She watches as Troy approaches Len but doesn't shake hands with him. She can't know that her Tupperware man is defending her honor.

"Thank you for being such a dolt that you passed on Giselle," he tells the country & western star. "She's everything to me. Extraordinary, and the rest."

Upon hearing this endorsement from another man, Len is suddenly filled with panic, and the knowledge that he must have Giselle back. When he later corners her in front of the Stairway to Heaven ride, she backs away as if from a ledge.

"What do you want?" Giselle asks.

"To see you."

"Len, after you I vowed never again to have my insides snipped apart like Grand Opening ribbons. So go on back to your little lackey." She means Mabel, the T-shirt girl.

"You got the 'lack' part right."

"Len, please go away."

"I can't. Giselle, when I lost you, it's as if all the glamour went out of my life."

"G-glamour?" Giselle stumbles, feeling suddenly at sea. "But I don't even comb my hair."

"Come on," says Len, advancing on her. "Now you know as well as I do, that's not what glamour is."

Troy emerges jubilantly, arms in the air, having just completed the ride, and Giselle quickly leaves Len to greet him. Together they go on to meet newlyweds Strood and Brad, Violet waving like a sailor soon to commence shore leave.

"Giselle, I just ran into Sidonia. She told me Adon and Whitney have just gotten married!"

"God, it's like a contagious disease. Oh, I'm sorry, I didn't mean... I thought Sidonia only did travel writing now?"

"She does. She was doing this piece on prison towns and she was in Soledad at the same time as the happy couple were tying the knot. She also told me there's a letter in a teen magazine about Adon having some irons in the fire."

"Well, since he's fired me, the irons he has are likely to be the kind most people use as doorstops. Paperweights. Honestly, it's as if my entire client roster has suddenly gone giddy with free will. Where did you see Sidonia?"

"Over by the Love Potion Number Nine booth. By the way, guess who's Madame Rue."

"Xenia."

"Got in it one."

"Excuse me, I'll just go and have a word with her," says Giselle, who finds Xenia but not Sidonia. The psychic explains she's had a vision of where Frances Culligan is. "Zabriskie Point in Death Valley," she intones and Giselle is suddenly seized with the realization that she must go there, must put a missing little girl before her work.

"She *is* your work," Violet Strood says later, over coffee in the Sugar Shack. "I don't mean to rain on your altruism, but it happens to be true."

Troy regrets he'll be unable to go with Giselle because he has a full slate of Tupperware events in the next few days.

"Hey, I'll drive you," says Brad to Strood's disbelief. "I've always loved that Antonioni flick."

The word "flick" makes Strood wince so intensely, she almost induces her impending labor.

In the lounge of the Furnace Creek Inn, Giselle tells Brad she's sure Zabriskie Point, where they'd hiked earlier, wandering around its partitions like office employees in search of a water cooler, was little more than a red herring.

"I don't think Xenia knows what she's doing any more, now that she's gone legit," Giselle says, demoralized. "My own feeling is that Frances is in some kind of High Sierra cabin hideaway. I just hope she's okay."

"I'm sure she's fine," purrs Brad, putting his alluvial palm over Giselle's twig-like fingers. "Why don't we go up to our room now?"

"Rooms. We each have our own."

"I just don't want to be alone. No strings—I just want to hold you."

"Don't tell me, your wife doesn't understand you."

"That's just it. She does understand me. That's the problem." As Brad leans in to kiss her, Giselle stands up abruptly, her chair scraping the parquet floor. "I'll see you in the morning," she says, although it's only just dusk. "Don't you dare knock on my door."

When she hears a tapping later that evening, Giselle pretends she's asleep, though sleep will elude her like a closed rest area off a tedious four-lane. "If I get through this," she tells herself, "I'll firmly believe in life after Death Valley."

When they meet the next morning in the lobby, Brad looks like he's slept in a chair, in his clothes. "I'm a father," he announces almost apologetically. "Violet's had a girl."

"Congratulations." As she goes to check out, the clerk at the counter tells her there was a call for her the previous night. "I knocked on your door but you must have been out." Giselle reads the message. *Pandra here. Rory, too. Xenia now thinks the Culligan girl is in Reno—had a dream of her standing below the Biggest Little City in the World sign.*

"Looks like I'm going to Reno," she tells Brad. "Can you give me a lift to a car-rental place?"

Adon is in the Sundowner Casino in Reno, toasting his bride, Whitney, with his third party hat–shaped glass. "I don't know what they put in martinis," he says, "but...." Before he can finish, if it was his intention to finish, Whitney spies her daughter a few feet away, accompanied by two fashionably dressed young women.

"Frances!" she calls.

"Go away!" the child shouts. "My name's Tania now, and these are my new moms." She gestures to Janine and Herm-ione who stand perfectly still.

"Suit yourself," Whitney replies. "I raised you to make your own decisions."

"I'm getting Spike back, too," the little girl adds. "He's mine—not yours."

Giselle wears a leopard-print jersey pantsuit as she sits in the noisy lobby of her Reno hotel. From her vantage point, she can read the sign on the marquee across the narrow street. "One night only *LEN TINGLE*. Prime Rib $4.95."

Len walks in through the automatic doors alone, a suitcase in one hand, guitar case in the other, St. Valentine's Day Mas-sacre–style. Trailing him on a leash is Kachina.

He detours from the path to the desk to approach Giselle.

"Where's your girlfriend?" she asks.

"We split up."

"Oh. Why?"

"Because she wasn't you."

Giselle closes her tired eyes, the lids coursing with eyeliner. She tries to catch and contain her tears.

"Let me take care of this business," Len says. "Could you look after Kachina?" The dog jumps into her leopard lap, as if seeking to be gently enfolded by a predator.

In his room Len has a steep erection which Giselle ignores, preferring him to give her deep and languorous oral sex. "Render me unable to walk," she whispers, in part to redress the balance for the times she'd pleasured him and he'd patted her on the head like an obedient puppy.

When he stands up, it's he who trips, on Giselle's lamé stiletto spring-o-later. As she sleeps, Len writes a song he'll call "We Know Reno." When she awakens, he sits on the bed. "I love you," he says. "I love you. Once for did, twice for do."

"Well, I hate you."

"If you hate me so much, why don't you marry me?"

"I don't want to be married. Why are you here with me?"

Len sighs. "I missed who you thought I was."

Giselle says finally, "Maybe I like what I see through."

"I'd give you a diamond."

"As big as the Ritz?"

"As big as a Ritz cracker."

In a coffee shop, Giselle and Len swivel in the low-backed vinyl chairs.

"A stack with Vermont, and a blonde with sand," Len tells the waitress.

"Make that two."

"Coming right up."

And their happiness hangs, waving and flagging on a short-order cook's baroque silver-plated carousel.

THE END

ABOUT THE AUTHOR

Susan Compo is the author of two collections of
stories, *Life After Death* and *Malingering*. She lives in
Los Angeles, and teaches in the Professional Writing
Program at the University of Southern California.

ALSO AVAILABLE FROM VERSE CHORUS PRESS

The Last Rock Star Book, or: Liz Phair, a Rant
BY CAMDEN JOY

Camden Joy's hero can charm landladies, but he can't seem to wrap up the quickie bio of rock star Liz Phair he's been commissioned to write. Instead, the shaky author finds himself recounting the troubled events that mark his own life. His ex-girlfriend (who just might be the illegitimate daughter of dead Rolling Stone Brian Jones); the rock star (whom he's never met); and a mystery girl in an old newspaper photo all start to blur together.

If only he could get closer to his subject, before the assignment spins out of control, maybe he'd have a shot at the distinction he deserves. Hilarious and compelling, *The Last Rock Star Book* offers both an engrossing read and a powerful meditation on celebrity and obsession.

"Pop culture obsessives will hear echoes of all sorts in Joy's voice—ecstatic art seraphs Patti Smith and Allen Ginsberg, Greil Marcus and Lester Bangs—not to mention the wild cadences of crank religious missives. It makes you lust for a world of heightened feelings and values beyond the one we live in—just like art is supposed to do."—MINNEAPOLIS CITY PAGES

$14.95. Paperback. 212 pages. ISBN 1-891241-07-9

Great Pop Things:
The Real History of Rock and Roll from Elvis to Oasis
BY COLIN B. MORTON & CHUCK DEATH *(introduction by Greil Marcus)*

These comic strips deliver an irreverent and devastatingly funny history of rock and roll. Like Monty Python, their version is surreal and ridiculous, yet somehow everything in it rings true. According to *Great Pop Things*, "despite having been able to think up brilliant titles for their first three albums, Led Zeppelin were stuck for what to call the fourth one—so they put a load of prunes on the front." As for Brian Eno, it was only after he was struck by a cab one day that he invented "ambivalent music, which you can't quite tell if you are listening to or not."

In strip after strip, Morton & Death pinpoint the absurdities and oddities of rock history. In the process, they often come closer to its truth than most conventional accounts, as well as being far more entertaining.

"Imagine a deeply knowledgeable, highly insightful rock history penned by the staff of Mad magazine.... Sure, it's just a comic strip, but Great Pop Things is music criticism at its confrontational best."—ENTERTAINMENT WEEKLY

$16.95. Paperback. 232 pages. ISBN 1-891241-08-7

Scraps
PHOTOGRAPHS BY MICHAEL GALINSKY

Noted rock photographer and musician Michael Galinsky spent years touring the country with his band Sleepyhead—and he always had his camera close to hand. *Scraps* is a collection of black-and-white photos that document the places he's seen, floors they've crashed on, bands they've played with—plus friends and strangers they met along the way in the underground-music community. Galinsky's photographs merit comparison both to Robert Frank's "on the road" images in *The Americans* and to Nan Goldin's candid portraits of her intimate circle. Those depicted include Sonic Youth, Bikini Kill, Yo La Tengo, Rodan, Come, Beat Happening, the Make Up, Kicking Giant, Slant 6, and more.

Many of Galinsky's peers contributed rare/unreleased recordings to an 18-song CD that accompanies the book. The artists include Yo La Tengo, Dump, Ruby Falls, Two Dollar Guitar, Sleepyhead, Antietam, Kicking Giant, and Fuck.

Co-published by Tract Home Publications and Sugar Free Records

$19.95. paperback + CD. ISBN 1-891241-09-5

Highway to Hell: The Life & Times of AC/DC Legend Bon Scott
BY CLINTON WALKER

Since its initial publication in Australia, *Highway to Hell* has established itself as a classic of rock writing. It's the definitive account of AC/DC's rise to fame, covering the years in which the band conceived their highly influential brand of rock'n'roll based on the formidable crosscut riffing of guitarists Angus and Malcolm Young and the ribald lyrics and charismatic stage presence of singer Bon Scott.

Drawing on first-person interviews and featuring many rare photos, *Highway to Hell* traces AC/DC's career through the life of their original front man, from the Scottish roots he shared with the Youngs to small-time gigs to recording studios and international success—right up to Scott's shocking death in 1980, just as the band had attained the worldwide recognition for which they'd worked so tirelessly.

AC/DC's abiding superstar status—and their influence on such different genres as hard rock, grunge, and rap-metal—ensure that Bon Scott's presence continues to be felt. Now *Highway to Hell* offers a fitting tribute to a seminal rock figure.

"A timely and acclaimed biography."—BILLBOARD

"A well-written and thoroughly researched biography... sensitive but unsentimental.—Q

"Bon Scott was possibly the most likeable rogue ever to walk the earth, and Clinton Walker paints a vivid picture of not just the man but also the machinations of being in a rock band.—WHO WEEKLY (AUSTRALIA)

$22.95. Paperback. 318 pages. ISBN 1-891241-13-3

ALSO BY CLINTON WALKER:

Stranded: The Secret History of Australian Independent Music, 1977-1991

An authoritative account of Australian punk and new wave from that country's leading music critic. Featuring the Saints, Radio Birdman, the Go-Betweens, the Birthday Party, the Scientists, the Triffids, Nick Cave, and many more.

$12.95. paperback. 346 pages

AVAILABLE FROM VERSE CHORUS PRESS